Acting Edition

I0591574

Ken Ludwig's
The Gods of
Comedy

‖SAMUEL FRENCH‖

FOR PRODUCTION INQUIRIES

UNITED STATES AND CANADA
info@concordtheatricals.com
1-866-979-0447

UNITED KINGDOM AND EUROPE
licensing@concordtheatricals.co.uk
020-7054-7298

Each title is subject to availability from Concord Theatricals Corp., depending upon country of performance. Please be aware that KEN LUDWIG'S THE GODS OF COMEDY may not be licensed by Concord Theatricals Corp. in your territory. Professional and amateur producers should contact the nearest Concord Theatricals Corp. office or licensing partner to verify availability.

MUSIC AND THIRD-PARTY MATERIALS USE NOTE

IMPORTANT BILLING AND CREDIT REQUIREMENTS

KEN LUDWIG'S THE GODS OF COMEDY was first produced by McCarter Theatre Center (Emily Mann, Artistic Director; Michael S. Rosenberg, Managing Director) in Princeton, New Jersey on March 12, 2019. The production was directed by Amanda Dehnert, with sets by Jason Sherwood, costumes by Linda Roethke, lights by Brian Gale, sound by Darron L West, wigs and makeup by Carissa Thorlakson, and illusions by Jim Steinmeyer. The production stage manager was Cheryl Mintz.

KEN LUDWIG'S THE GODS OF COMEDY was produced in association with The Old Globe (Barry Edelstein, Artistic Director; Timothy J. Shields, Managing Director) in San Diego, California on May 11, 2019. The production was directed by Amanda Dehnert, with sets by Jason Sherwood, costumes by Linda Roethke, lights by Brian Gale, sound by Darron L West, wigs and makeup by Carissa Thorlakson, choreography by Ellenore Scott, and illusions by Jim Steinmeyer. The production stage manager was Alison Cote. The cast was as follows:

ARISTIDE / ALEKSI / ARES . . . . .George Psomas
DAPHNE . . . . .Shay Vawn
DEAN TRICKETT . . . . Keira Naughton
RALPH . . . . Jevon McFerrin
ZOE / BROOKLYN. . . . . Steffanie Leigh
DIONYSUS. . . . . Brad Oscar
THALIA . . . . .Jessie Cannizzaro

CHARACTERS

7 Actors: 4 women, 3 men

ARISTIDE

DAPHNE

DEAN TRICKETT

RALPH

ZOE

ALEKSI

DIONYSUS

THALIA

BROOKLYN

ARES

SETTING

The bulk of the action takes place on a college campus.

TIME

The present.

AUTHOR'S NOTE

The Gods of Comedy is dear to my heart for a number of reasons.

As a student, I was insufferably academic. I was drawn to literature, music and art the way a bee is drawn to honey, and no matter what other disciplines I explored, the attraction to the arts was undeniable. It was part of my DNA. From age eight onwards, I read everything I could lay my hands on; I studied music incessantly (I became, and remain, an enormous fan of Italian bel canto opera); I tried sculpture until I realized I wasn't very good at it; I read thousands of plays (knowing from an early age that I wanted to go into the theater); and by age fifteen, Homer's *The Odyssey* was my favorite book.

What could better ignite a young scholar's love of literature than the works of Homer? The literary critic Northrop Frye says that all scholars are either *Iliad* critics or *Odyssey* critics, depending on their predisposition to tragedy or comedy. I was always drawn more to *The Odyssey* thanks to an inborn love of comedy that I still can't explain.

Looking back, it would have been grand to have been a Classics major in college and learned to read ancient Greek so that I would now have a shot at reading *The Odyssey* in the original. As it worked out, I double-majored in English Literature and Music Theory; but in my Junior year I took a course in Greek Literature in Translation from the great Classics scholar Richmond Lattimore. At that time, Lattimore's translations of Homer, Aeschylus, Sophocles, and Euripides were the standard texts for ancient Greek literature in the English-speaking world.

(Once, as a Junior, I had the temerity of inviting Lattimore to a play I'd written for Class Nite – the night of bacchanalian revelry where each class wrote and produced a play lampooning the faculty. Mine involved a Mexican village, a whorehouse, and a church, and by the end of the evening, the shy and self-effacing Professor Lattimore was rolling his eyes and looking at me as though I was insane.)

Fast forward twenty-five years, and I was sitting in my study thinking about what to write next, when I turned and picked up the wonderful new translation of *The Odyssey* by Emily Wilson. First I read the terrific Introduction and Translator's Note. Then I continued to the text itself, and within one hundred lines, I was reading this:

> *With that, [Athena] tied her sandals on her feet,*
> *The marvelous golden sandals that she wears*
> *To travel sea and land, as fast as wind.*
> *She took the heavy bronze-tipped spear she uses*
> *to tame the ranks of the warriors with whom*
> *she is enraged. Then from the mountain down*
> *she sped to Ithaca, and stopped outside*

Odysseus' court, bronze spear in hand.
She looked like Mentes now, the Taphian leader,
a guest-friend.

Within a few more lines, Athena, in her disguise as Mentes, meets Telemachus, Odysseus' son, and Telemachus says:

Good evening,
stranger, and welcome. Be our guest, come and share
our dinner, and then tell us what you need.

And suddenly it struck me that here, in the ways of the Greek gods, was the kernel of a stage comedy.

To the ancients Greeks (at least as represented in their literature), the gods were always among us. The gods were not ghosts, visiting us from the past. And they didn't live in the skies or in some ethereal or psychological world that we couldn't see and feel. Greek gods were a bit like the heroes in the Marvel Universe. They lived nearby in different neighborhoods, and they joined us in our adventures at their will.

In the case of the gods of ancient Greece, they lived in a specific place: on Mount Olympus, which is a real geographical location on mainland Greece near Thessalonica. They kept an eye on our comings and goings; and whenever they felt the need or the desire, they stepped down off their mountain and mingled among us. We see this behavior in the early lines of *The Odyssey* that I just quoted, where Athena disguises herself as Mentes and joins Telemachus at his home in Ithaca. And we see it again and again throughout the two Homeric epics, then in Catullus and a myriad of other Greek sources.

So what struck me that day was the idea of writing a comedy set in the present where the gods of Olympus come down from their mountain to help a mortal who is in trouble. In the end, I named her Daphne and decided that she was having trouble with her career and her heart at the same time.

As the plot thickened, she became a Classics scholar who had just returned from a summer in Greece. And, being a Classics scholar, she calls on the gods of ancient Greece to help her in her troubled state, and lo and behold, they walk in the door. The trouble is that the two particular gods who come to help her are Dionysus and Thalia, the gods of Comedy. And being the gods of Comedy, as opposed to the gods of Wisdom or Tragedy, every time they try to help her, they manage to make matters worse. They just keep tripping over themselves despite their good intentions.

What struck me then and continues to nag at me whenever I think about the history of comedy (which is most of my waking hours, I'm ashamed to say) is why aren't more plays written about gods and other supernatural beings? What better place could there be than the theater to represent the extra-normal? Think of *A Midsummer Night's Dream*, where Shakespeare creates an entire fairy kingdom, and where Oberon, the King of the Fairies has merely to say, "I am invisible," and he becomes invisible right in front of us. Then, just two lines later, when other characters walk onstage and don't see him, he creates theater magic by being there (to the audience) and not being there (to the other players onstage) at the same time. Only in the theater could this stroke of genius be so effective.

I was also attracted by the idea of writing a play set in the modern world of Classical Literature as a kind of farce, because that's how comedy, at least in Western Literature, got its start. The first comic playwright in Western history was a Greek named Aristophanes, but his comic political surrealism never really caught on after his death in 386 BC. Two hundred years later came the first truly great comic playwright, Titus Maccius Plautus, a Roman who wrote in Latin, who more or less created dramatic comedy as we know it.

When we read Plautus, and certainly when we see him in production, we realize that his plays, though highly sophisticated, aren't primarily psychological studies of dramatic types, or implied comedies with roots in tragedy whose inheritor is Chekhov. Primarily, they're farces, filled with mistaken identity, old men longing for young women, young sons wanting to escape their parents, knockabout drubbings, verbal complications, pirates, courtesans, and lots of sex. It is no coincidence that early in his career, Shakespeare adapted one of Plautus's comedies, *Menaechmi*, and called it *The Comedy of Errors*.

This is all to say that in developing the idea of having two Greek gods come down to visit a modern-day mortal, it seemed entirely appropriate to set this comedy in the Classics Department of a liberal arts college where other-worldly hijinks felt especially natural.

I only hope that this play is a small but worthy addition to the tradition of stage comedies with other-worldly concerns like *Amphitryon*, *Blithe Spirit*, and *Visit to a Small Planet*, where visits from gods, ghosts and extraterrestrials adds to the likelihood of onstage joy.

"Let wonder seem familiar."
– William Shakespeare, *Much Ado About Nothing*
Act V, Scene Four

*"A mind might ponder its thoughts for ages and not gain so much
self-knowledge as the passion of love shall teach it in a day."*
– Ralph Waldo Emerson, *Essays: History*

For my brother, Gene,
the best man in the world,
my model in all things,
and a God of Comedy in his own right.

And with thanks to Temple Wright
of the Harvard Center for Hellenic Studies
for his trusty advice.

ACT I

Scene One

(We're at a bazaar on the island of Naxos in Greece in the present day. The sounds of the marketplace fill the air, including the cries of street vendors and the rumble of traffic going by on the street.)

*(**DAPHNE RAIN** is sitting at a café table amid stacks of books and papers, deeply immersed in her scholarship. She's an American academic in her mid-twenties.)*

*(Nearby, we see **ARISTIDE**, wearing a traditional Greek robe and fez. He speaks English with a Greek accent.)*

ARISTIDE. *(To the audience.)* Welcome to Naxos, island of myth and legend. It was here that Zeus, the King of the Gods, was born in a cave not half a league from this very spot. On that day, the earth trembled, the skies broke apart – and to celebrate this event, I sell you souvenirs at a very good price.

> *(He flashes the inside of his vest, which is hung with trinkets like the ones on his souvenir cart nearby.)*

(To someone in the audience.) Madam, this bracelet is made from gemstones forged in the caves of the Titans themselves and the price is only –

> *(No sale.)*

You sir, these pearls are treasures of the Aegean Sea, found by local divers who plunge into the sparkling waters of the...

(No sale.)

(To himself.) Hoo boy, this is tough crowd.

DAPHNE. *(To herself, reading from her computer.)* "Ancient Myths and Modern Voices, by Daphne Rain."

ARISTIDE. And there she is. The subject of tonight's entertainment.

DAPHNE. "For decades, the tomb paintings of Ancient Naxos have been a source of academic controversy with regard to their origins."

(She begins typing.)

ARISTIDE. Believe me, this is not the kind of romantic comedy halfwit you are used to meeting at a place like this *(i.e. the theater.)*. She is a scholar with the world at her feet. *(To **DAPHNE**.)* Excuse me, young lady, may I offer you a keepsake before you leave us on Sunday to return to America?

DAPHNE. How do you know I'm leaving Sunday?

ARISTIDE. Miss, please. I know everything that happens on my island kingdom. You are a Classics professor from the United States. You are here leading students for the summer, but you study too hard and you do not join them on their happy excursions. In addition, you worry too much, you lack confidence, you are up for tenure, and your mother is very concerned about you.

DAPHNE. Well that's not true.

(Ring! Her cell phone rings. She sees the display.)

Hello, Mother.

*(**ARISTIDE** shrugs as if to say, "Of course I'm right.")*

*(**DAPHNE**, embarrassed, turns and whispers into the phone.)*

Yes, Mother, I do have a life. Yes of course I have friends. I don't *need* a boyfriend, I need tenure. What's wrong with that? If I don't get tenure, I'll be teaching gym.

> *(Her mother says something, and she smiles happily but wistfully.)*

Yes, I know, Father loved it here. And I saw his book on Sophocles at the museum. ...Yeah, I miss him too.

DEAN TRICKETT. *(Offstage.) Daphne?*

DAPHNE. Oh no, it's my Dean. I have to go. But I'll see you next week. I'll come to visit. Love you too. Bye bye.

> *(As she hangs up, **DEAN TRICKETT** enters with a determined step. The **DEAN** is a force of nature.)*

> *(About fifty-five, she has a shock of grey hair and an English accent. She's happily and rather wildly ungainly and has the full-throated laugh of a large woodland creature.)*

DEAN. Daphne, there you are. Now listen to me. The new man – Professor Sargent – just arrived and he's driving me mad at the moment. He says he's on to something here in Naxos and needs someone to help him look through the library now, this minute, and he's driving me crazy!

RALPH. *(Offstage.)* Dean Trickett.

DEAN. Oh no, it's him. Hide me. Quick.

> *(She darts behind a rack of shawls on the souvenir stand and tries to hide, as **RALPH SARGENT** enters.)*

> *(He's a thirty-five year old American classicist with horn-rimmed glasses. He's bursting with energy and is very good looking.)*

RALPH. Dean Trickett?

DEAN. *(Caught.)* Oh, there you are.

RALPH. Have you had any luck yet?

DEAN. I'm afraid I haven't.

RALPH. Grk! Grk! Grk!

> *(This is an inarticulate sound that* **RALPH** *makes when he is angry.)*

DEAN. Professor Sargent, Miss Rain, who now thinks you're insane.

DAPHNE. How do you do.

DEAN. Miss Rain is an Instructor with the department, and I have great plans for her. She's putting on *Medea* with her students when we get back.

RALPH. Okay. Euripides. What do we know?

DEAN. One of the four greatest playwrights in the history of the world. How's that for starters?

DAPHNE. Fifth century BC, wrote ninety-five plays.

RALPH. Right. And how many of those plays survive?

DEAN. Very few indeed.

DAPHNE. Seventeen.

RALPH. Exactly. We have seven for Sophocles, seven for Aeschylus –

DEAN. And your tedious point about all this is?

RALPH. I'm on the trail of a new one, which is why I need help.

DAPHNE. A whole new play?

RALPH. No, no. I wish. "A play." But I have a lead on a fragment, and nobody's found more than a line of Euripides in a hundred years.

DAPHNE. What play is it from?

RALPH. *Andromeda.* It was written in

DAPHNE. 412 BC. Aristophanes talks about it, but it was lost.

RALPH. Exactly. But we do know a great deal about it. We know that it started with Andromeda chained to a rock as a human sacrifice. Ovid tells the story, and he says, quote:

"At this moment, the hero Perseus,
Slayer of the Gorgon, flew across the sky,
And at the sight of Andromeda on the watery cliff,
Her body white and naked from the foam,
Her arms in chains that cut her flesh like knives,
Sending rivers of blood across the marble of her
Arching back, he fell in love."

DAPHNE. *(Her voice rough.)* Whoa.

DEAN. Whoa.

ARISTIDE. Whoa.

RALPH. Now what's amazing here is that we think that it's the first play ever to portray two people

DAPHNE. falling in love onstage.

RALPH. Which means that it changed the entire course

DAPHNE & RALPH. of theater history.

DAPHNE. And you think the fragment is here in the library?

RALPH. No, I think it was *sent* from here –

DAPHNE. And the *records* of the shipment are here in Naxos.

RALPH. Right. Which is why I need some help, so what do you say?

DEAN. I say good luck to you. Live long and prosper. I have some very important *research* to do, so I'll see you later. *(Sotto voce, to* **DAPHNE.***)* Wild goose chase. See you on the beach.

> *(The* **DEAN** *exits.)*

RALPH. Do *you* have time?

DAPHNE. Me? No, I-I-I still have research to do. It's important.

RALPH. Right. Of course. Well thanks. It was nice meeting you.

> *(He exits.* **DAPHNE** *touches her precious books, feeling guilty, and* **ARISTIDE** *catches her eye.)*

ARISTIDE. Tsk tsk tsk.

DAPHNE. What?

ARISTIDE. Would you rather sit alone writing about tomb paintings or have an adventure with a handsome man involving a lost manuscript?

DAPHNE. Sit alone.

(**RALPH** *hurries back on.*)

RALPH. Sorry, I forgot my briefcase.

(*He retrieves his briefcase and starts to head off again.* **DAPHNE** *is tortured about what to do but* **ARISTIDE** *gives her a nudge.*)

DAPHNE. *Wait!* Actually, I-I suppose I could help if you really need it.

RALPH. Could you really? Can you start right now?

(*She looks at* **ARISTIDE**, *who nods.*)

DAPHNE. Yes. I-I guess I could. I'll just be a minute.

RALPH. Great! It's just down the street. I'll see you there!

(*He hurries off.*)

DAPHNE. Ohhh.

(*As* **DAPHNE** *gathers her papers together, we hear the roar of the nearby traffic on the street. Suddenly, she notices something a few yards away and hurries up to* **ARISTIDE**.)

Wait a second. The boy on the street, is that your son? Because a bus went by and I think he's going to get hurt if he doesn't move back a little –

ARISTIDE. *Nikki. Nicholas, get away from there.*

DAPHNE. Just last year my nephew was in a terrible accident and *oh my God*! *LOOK OUT!*

(**DAPHNE** *rushes away. Zoom! Honk, honk!*)

ARISTIDE. *NIKKI!*

ZOE. (*Running by.*) *NIKKI!*

ARISTIDE. *Oh my God!*

(**DAPHNE** *runs back in holding a bundle of clothing with* **NIKKI** *inside.* **ARISTIDE** *and his wife,* **ZOE**, *run in behind her. Honk! Zooooom!*)

NIKKI. *Whhhhaaaaaaaaaaaaaaaaa!*

DAPHNE. It's all right, you're okay. Here take him.

ZOE. *(Angry at* **ARISTIDE**.*) He could have been killed!*

ARISTIDE. *(To* **ZOE**.*)* Zoe! I'm sorry! Sig nómi!

ZOE. *Malaka! You are stupid!*

ARISTIDE. *I said I'm sorry!*

(*She storms away.*)

(*In shock.*) You have saved my son and I owe you his life.

DAPHNE. Oh I'm-I'm not sure of that –

ARISTIDE. Please choose what you like from my humble stand. You will do me honor. Here, take scarf of silk. Or gemstone ring or wait. I have something special put away.

(*He reaches into the back of his stand and pulls out a necklace with a disk of gold hanging from the bottom. The disk is carved with ancient symbols.*)

This is for you. It is talisman – a magic charm. When the holder of the charm is in need of help, he calls on the Gods of Ancient Greece and they save him no matter what he requires.

DAPHNE. Thank you.

ARISTIDE. Good luck, Miss Daphne Rain. There is a handsome young man waiting for you on the steps over there. He will not wait forever.

RALPH. *(Offstage.) Daphne! Hello?*

DAPHNE. *I'm coming!*

(*In a storm of disorder.*)

Books, a lot of books...

(*Running off with her books.*)

Thanks for the necklace! And take care of your son!

ARISTIDE. I will! Good luck!

> *(Dixieland music* strikes up as the set changes. The front curtain descends and it shows a map of the world – just the Western Hemisphere – with Greece on the far right and the United States on the left, with an* Indiana Jones-*type dotted line from Naxos to a city on the East Coast of the U.S.)*

> *(As the music plays,* **ARISTIDE** *acquires a stick with an airplane on the end and he traces the route of* **DAPHNE**'s *flight home.)*

And now we follow the aeroplane of this fine young woman as she flies from here in Naxos, first to Athens, then to Malta, and then out across the Mediterranean Sea, high above Tunisia, Algeria, Morocco, and then, *whoop!*, she heads northward, over Southern Spain – and I ask you, who in this room does not love Granada? – and then *whoosh!*, she is soaring high above the Atlantic Ocean like a goddess herself, *vroom*, the engines are purring like a thousand kittens, *mmmmmmm*, but then, oh no, the turbulence hits them and the plane flies high then low then south then north to avoid the thunderstorm which could be Zeus who is angry at these mortals flying by like gods! – but then, at last, *ahoy*, America beckons. But as she approaches her destination, she has a layover first in Baltimore because she has purchased the cheapest ticket available and the poor girl's legroom is nonexistent. But then the plane lifts off again, and soon our heroine is cruising into her final stop, Newark Airport, where her plane is setting down like the gentle winds themselves, returning to their mother earth, and so her journey ends in safety and peace. Thank you for listening.

---

* A license to produce *The Gods of Comedy* does not include a performance license for any third-party or copyrighted music. Licensees should create an original composition or use music in the public domain. For further information, please see Music Use Note on page 3.

Scene Two

(A month later. We're in the faculty office of the Classics Department of an American liberal arts college, which is housed in a comfortable nineteenth century house at the edge of campus. The room is sunny, friendly, filled with books and contains a sofa and chairs, as well as a desk and some office equipment.)

*(**DAPHNE** is consulting her notes.)*

DAPHNE. "Note for the Program: For over two thousand years, Euripides' *Medea* has held a shifting place in the consciousness of the play-going public. In the nineteenth century it was seen as a call to arms for women's rights, and it is now considered an icon of modern feminism. In this context, focus has centered on Medea's predicament as a wife rejected for a younger woman, and as a mother whose children are used as a weapon in the war of the sexes, as when she cries in her most famous speech:

> *(She starts small, but her passion grows as she recites the words until, by the end, she is a tiger with a spotlight shining down on her:)*

Death! Death! Death is my desire for myself and my children.
O how I wish that I might see Jason and his accursed bride
In utter ruin for all the wrongs that they have done me!
O Vengeance!
Oh I know you think me a timid creature in the main,
A coward who will never stand her ground and fight,
But shine on me the light of justice, and of hope,
And by the gods I swear I will not fail!"

ALEKSI. *(Clapping.)* Bravo! Bravo!

(The lights change, and we now see **ALEKSI**, *the custodian, in the doorway with his wheely cart that holds a broom and a plastic bag for trash.)*

*(***ALEKSI** *is a Russian émigré who speaks with a gentle Russian accent.)*

DAPHNE. *Ahh!* Oh, Aleksi, you scared me.

ALEKSI. You are beink magnificent in this role, Miss Rain. You will be tremendous.

DAPHNE. Thanks but I'm just directing. I couldn't play it in front of all those people.

ALEKSI. Why not? To me you are lion. And you have a feelink for this Medea woman, as though she is somewhere deep inside you.

DAPHNE. She does some awful things, you know.

ALEKSI. But she *does* them. She does not play by the rules.

DAPHNE. How do you know so much about the Greeks?

ALEKSI. I have always admired them. In St. Petersburg we are sailors, like the Greeks, and we especially admire Odysseus for protecting his shipmates from the peril of the sea, then returning to his wife on the sands of Ithaca. *"O sing to me, Muse, of the man of twists and turns, who plundered the hallowed heights of Troy."* Oh Miss Rain, our lives are pale in comparison to these people.

DAPHNE. You're the one who should be in the play.

ALEKSI. Now that would be something. But for now I will keep my steady job and come back to clean this room when you are not so busy.

DAPHNE. I'll only be a few more minutes.

(Calling to him as he exits.)

Thank you, Aleksi!

(Ring! The phone rings.)

Hello, Classics Department. Oh Catherine, hi. Can you imagine? It's only a week till we give the first performance –

(She hears something awful and staggers backward.)

What? Two actors?! You're kidding me. They can't just leave the show like that, it's one week away! And it's my translation!

(She takes a breath and gathers herself.)

Okay, listen. Put notices on all the bulletin boards and call me back.

(She hangs up the phone.)

Ahhh. What is the matter with these people?

(RALPH stumbles in, carrying his briefcase. He's in a daze, but somehow gets to a chair and sits down. He has a faraway look in his eyes, and can't speak.)

Hi. Do you want to hear something infuriating? Two of my actors for *Medea* just quit. Like that. And I can't just find two actors overnight.

(RALPH hasn't moved or reacted.)

Ralph? Ralph, what's the matter? And what are you doing back so soon? I thought you were getting close on the –...

(No answer. And then it dawns on her.)

Did you find something? Oh my God, you found the fragment, didn't you. Did you find a whole page?

(He looks up at her.)

You found a page, right?

(He shakes his head no.)

Did you find a few lines at least? How many? Five? Three?

(No response.)

Ralph, say something!

RALPH. I found the whole play.

(Stunned silence.)

DAPHNE. *(Quietly.) Andromeda*?

RALPH. I can't... I can't breathe. *(Gasp.)* I'm serious. *(Gasp.)* Do something. *(Gasp.)* Oh my God, I can't breathe.

DAPHNE. Shall I call an ambulance? I'll call an ambulance!

RALPH. No!

DAPHNE. *What?!*

RALPH. Water. I need some water.

DAPHNE. Right. I-I've got it. Here it is. Drink. Better? Better? *Is it better?!*

RALPH. *Yes, I think so!*

DAPHNE. Sorry.

> *(He's breathing now.)*

How did you find it?

RALPH. I-I-I narrowed it down to...

DAPHNE. to the college, yes, I know –

RALPH. and I went to the stacks thinking well, if there is a fragment, it must have been miscatalogued, so instead of going to the Greek section, I went to the History section, and looked at the As for Andromeda: first A, then A-N, then A-N-D, and then I saw this bundle of papers behind some books, and there it was.

> *(With reverence, he takes the book out of his briefcase. It looks very old. The cover is worn, and the pages are loose because the binding gave way long ago. It is handwritten, a product of the European monasteries of the Middle Ages when ancient books were copied by monks.)*

DAPHNE. May I?

> *(She touches one of the pages and it makes her dizzy.)*

RALPH. I read it through and I think it's – ...

DAPHNE. What?

RALPH. I think it's a masterpiece. Listen to this, this is the opening:

"Oh Nyx hierah
hōhs mahkrón hippeumah diohkays
ahsteraydéa nohtah diphreuoos
aithéros hieráhs
too semnotáhtoo d'Olumpoo." *

DAPHNE. "O sacred night, beloved of Mystery,
How long is your chariot's path
Through the sky of stars,
Through the holy land of the Gods, Olympus."
It's so beautiful.

RALPH. It makes me cry.

DAPHNE. Me too.

RALPH. Euripides wrote it in his seventies, and when he died, Sophocles dressed the Chorus of his latest play in mourning out of respect for his beloved colleague.

DAPHNE. *(Hushed.)* Oh, Ralph, you'll be famous.

RALPH. Will I? Oh my God. Oh my God, oh my God!

> *(He jumps up and down. He punches the air. Then suddenly their faces are only inches apart. Obviously he wants to kiss her, but hesitates; so she kisses him. Then:)*

DAPHNE. Oh, I'm so happy for you.

> *(He explodes with joy.)*

RALPH. Ha ha! Listen! Could you do me a favor? I called Dean Trickett and told her that something exciting happened and I'd meet her in her office, so I need a favor. Would you hold this for me until I get back? I don't want to carry it around campus.

DAPHNE. You trust me with it?

RALPH. Of course I trust you. I'd trust you with anything. But I've got to go. Keep it safe. I'm going. Don't move.

---

* Ὦ Νὺξ ἱερά,
  ὡς μακρὸν ἵππευμα διώκεις
ἀστεροειδέα νῶτα διφρεύουσ'
αἰθέρος ἱερᾶς
  τοῦ σεμνοτάτου δι' 'Ολύμπου.

I'll be right back. Stay here. Don't move. Keep it safe.
Don't move. Hahaaaaa!

> (**RALPH** *kisses* **DAPHNE**. *Then he runs out.
> We hear him scream with happiness from
> offstage.* **DAPHNE** *is stunned. She holds the
> book to her chest. It's the treasure of the
> century.*)

DAPHNE. Oh my God.

> (*Ding dong! The doorbell rings. She squeezes
> the book as if it's a child, then puts the book
> on the desk and hurries out the door.*)

Coming!

> (*The instant she's gone,* **ALEKSI** *walks in with
> his cart.*)

ALEKSI. Hello? Miss Rain? Are you still here? Good. She is
gone.

> (*He begins cleaning the room, and by
> accident, his cart hits the desk and the
> manuscript falls into a trash can. He does not
> see this happen. A moment later, he notices
> that the trash can is full.*)

Puh. Look at this trash. It is good thing I am being
here, it is disgraceful.

> (*He empties the trash – including the
> manuscript – into the cart.*)

And look at this book. It is very old. No wonder they are
throwing it away. Wait. I have idea. I have been dying
to try the paper shredder since the day I got here! Oh,
just look at this baby. It is vintage.

> (*He turns on the shredder and we hear the
> loud whir of its gears. Whrrrrrrrrr!*)

OK, here goes.

> (*He tears a page from the manuscript and
> feeds it into the shredder. Grshhhhhhhunk!!
> It's shredded.*)

I am liking the very idea of shredder because it is philosophical. It say to me that life is fragile, and that which endures in this crazy world is only love and trust, not ink and paper.

(Grshhhhhhhhunk!! He shreds the second page.)

Wait. I am getting new idea. In the English Department there is even better shredder, which is doing three pages at the same time! I will shred the whole book in fifteen minutes! Haha!

*(**ALEKSI** exits. At which moment **DAPHNE** and the **DEAN** hurry in.)*

DEAN. He said he was *very* excited, and I just couldn't bear to wait any longer.

DAPHNE. Well I know he'll want to tell you himself because it's quite a find and he thinks of it as...

(She sees the empty spot on the desk where she left the manuscript and freezes. Then she staggers backward. During the following she looks around the desk, picks up other books and papers, looking everywhere.)

DEAN. As what?

DAPHNE. Hmm?

DEAN. You said he thinks of it "*as.*"

DAPHNE. Yes, ma'am.

DEAN. As what?

DAPHNE. As what?

DEAN. Yes.

DAPHNE. Of course.

DEAN. *Of course what?*

DAPHNE. Yes.

DEAN. *Yes what?! Daphne!*

(And now she's tearing the place apart, looking through shelves, under chairs, and behind the pillows.)

DEAN. Daphne, what are you doing?! You said he wanted to tell me himself and then you said that he thinks of it as –

DAPHNE. What's your extension?

DEAN. You know I am completely confused by –

DAPHNE. *(Grabbing her by the shoulders and shaking her.) WHAT'S YOUR EXTENSION?!*

DEAN. Three two eight.

DAPHNE. *(Runs to the phone and dials.)* Three two eight. Hello? Ralph? No, the Dean's here, only I wanted to ask you hmm? "How does it look?" The book? It looks magnificent. It's like *Gone With the Wind*, only it really is.

> *(She hangs up.)*

He's waiting for you.

DEAN. My dear, whatever it is, take heart. It's a college. If you weren't slightly insane, you wouldn't be here at all.

> *(She exits. **DAPHNE** is very still for a moment. Her heart has stopped beating and she starts to cry.)*

DAPHNE. Oh what'll I do? *What'll I do?!*

> *(She sobs so hard it hurts and she puts her hand on her chest to stop herself. There she feels the necklace with the charm that **ARISTIDE** gave her in Naxos. She grabs it fiercely.)*

Oh save me, Gods of Ancient Greece!

> *(And she runs from the room. Then suddenly we **hear epic motion picture theme music at full blast***. *It is stirring, full of blaring trumpets and great excitement. A shaft of light appears, then a puff of smoke – and enter the* **GODS OF COMEDY**, **DIONYSUS** *and*

THALIA. *They wear Greek robes and pose with magnificence.)*

(Before we go on: **DIONYSUS** *is one of the twelve Olympians of the Hellenic pantheon. He is not only the God of Comedy, he is also the God of Wine and Revelry. The ancient epics describe him as "a joy for mortals," but he is also the God of Misrule, with a hearty appetite for all things sexual. He is a son of Zeus and has been depicted in art by everyone from Michelangelo to Picasso. His tastes are boisterous, he is innately anarchic, and he loves the good life. Best of all, he's an enthusiast. He is the God of Exstasis, of being outside yourself. He is also extremely lovable and fun to be with.)*

*(***THALIA***, meanwhile, is seriously beautiful and seriously sexy. She is everything that men dream about but pretend they don't. She is technically a Muse, which is a kind of demi-goddess. There are nine Muses in Greek mythology, and she is the Muse of Comedy and Idyllic Poetry. Her mother, Mnemosyne, is the Goddess of Memory (see the portrait by Dante Gabriel Rossetti) and her eight sisters include Clio (History), Melpomene (Tragedy), Polyhymnia (Song), and Terpsichore (Dance). While she is not exactly the sharpest sword in the armory, she makes up for it with her wonderful self-confidence. She's beautiful, joyous and full of charm.)*

DIONYSUS. Welcome!
THALIA. To us!
DIONYSUS. For we
THALIA. are the Gods
DIONYSUS. of Comedy!

DIONYSUS & THALIA. Ta daaaaa!

(Confetti bursts out brilliantly behind them.)

DIONYSUS. And wait! Methinks a maiden is in distress in this kingdom.

THALIA. And methinks we can helpeth her and aideth her if we do findeth her and pityeth her.

DIONYSUS. Which we willeth.

THALIA. No doubteth.

DIONYSUS. Yea, verily.

DIONYSUS & THALIA. And we shall act like *gods*!

(They pose, then glance up at the heavens.)

THALIA. Psst!

DIONYSUS. Yeah?

THALIA. D'ya think Zeus, *(Calling heavenward.)* THE REMARKABLE MASTER OF ALL THE GODS *(To* **DIONYSUS.***)* is still watchin' us?

DIONYSUS. Nope, he's gone.

THALIA. Oh, thank goodness. He is such a challenge.

DIONYSUS. Scroll, please.

THALIA. Yes, sir.

(She pulls out the scroll.)

DIONYSUS. *(Reading.)* "Decree from Zeus, God of all the Heavens and the Earth: To the Gods of Comedy, Dionysus and Thalia. Subject: Daphne Rain."

THALIA. "Instructions: This mortal woman is frightened of heart, closed of mind, and she needs to unleash the gods from within. Therefore, your task is to give this woman"

DIONYSUS & THALIA. "an adventure and a happy ending."

THALIA. "Succeed and you shall prosper forever."

DIONYSUS. "Fail and you shall burn in Hades until your flesh and sinews are steaming red and ulcerous to the touch and you shall be banished forever from the sight of Olympus. Cordially yours, Zeus Almighty."

THALIA. I just hope we get it right this time.

DIONYSUS. I beg your pardon.

THALIA. It gets discouraging.

DIONYSUS. What are you – ...? Are we ever wrong about anything?

THALIA. Oh, please. Abraham Lincoln?

DIONYSUS. He was tense. He needed a good laugh.

THALIA. "There's a wonderful new play tonight at Ford's Theater, Mr. President."

DIONYSUS. Hey, it was worth a shot.

THALIA. And Napoleon?

DIONYSUS. What?

THALIA. You bet against him.

DIONYSUS. He was four feet tall. He surprised everybody.

THALIA. Oh Di, if we don't get this one right, we're in a lot of trouble. Zeus says he'll banish us forever.

DIONYSUS. No more nectar.

THALIA. No more ambrosia.

DIONYSUS. No more chicken bones in a little circle.

DAPHNE. *(Offstage.)* Hello?

THALIA. Shh. Somebody's comin'. It could be her.

(They pose. **DAPHNE** *enters.)*

DAPHNE. Hello? Can I help you with something?

DIONYSUS. Are you Daphne Rain?

DAPHNE. Yes, I am.

DIONYSUS. Then the question is, can we help you?

DIONYSUS & THALIA. Ta daaaaa!

DAPHNE. I just don't – oh. Oh I *see*. You're *actors*. How did you hear about it so quickly?

THALIA. I was sittin' by the Stream of Cadmus drying my nails when Hermes, Master of Cunning, dashes up and cries, "You've got a mission!" And then by accident he falls in the stream and I pull him out.

DIONYSUS. That was very brave for a Muse.

THALIA. Thanks. I like to think of myself as a eunuch.

DIONYSUS. A eunuch?

THALIA. Yeah. You know. Like one of a kind.

DIONYSUS. It's pronounced "unique."

THALIA. Oh yeah.

DIONYSUS. Lovely girl.

DAPHNE. Alright, here's the problem. I need two actors to be in *Medea*. One plays Jason and the other plays Medea and doubles as the Nurse.

THALIA. Oh I love playin' nurses! "Now don't you worry, Mr. Gottlieb, I brought your *rectal* thermometer!"

DIONYSUS. It's not that kind of nurse.

THALIA. Oh.

DAPHNE. Look, I'm sure you'd like to audition properly –

THALIA. We have to audition?

DIONYSUS. It has come to this.

DAPHNE. But I don't have time! I'm in a terrible mess, and I just can't help you!

> *(She starts to cry. She sobs. She can't stop herself.)*

THALIA. Help us? But we're here to help *you*. That's what we do.

DIONYSUS. We fix things.

THALIA. Like broken hearts

DIONYSUS. and shattered dreams.

THALIA. We deal with shipwrecked twins who keep missin' each other.

DIONYSUS. And old fat men who hide in laundry baskets.

THALIA. Pants roles,

DIONYSUS. sex,

THALIA. disguise,

DIONYSUS. sex,

THALIA. confusion.

DIONYSUS. sex.

THALIA. Enough with the sex!

DIONYSUS. But sex is funny.

THALIA. It is with you.

DAPHNE. Look, I'm sorry, you seem like very nice people, but I think you should go now. I'm – I'm in the middle of a – kind of a...

(*She chokes back a sob.*)

THALIA. Aw, don't cry, we can fix it, I promise.

DAPHNE. How can you *fix* it! *You can't fix it! I've ruined everything!*

(*She sobs and* **THALIA** *holds her.*)

THALIA. (*Over* **DAPHNE**'s *head.*) Do you want to tell her?

DIONYSUS. You do it.

THALIA. We can fix it because we're the Gods of Comedy.

DIONYSUS & THALIA. Ta daaaa!

DAPHNE. What do you mean?

DIONYSUS. (*Imitating* **DAPHNE**, *raising his hands and shaking his fingers.*) "Oh save me, Gods of Ancient Greece."

DAPHNE. (*Horrified.*) You-you were listening at the window.

THALIA. No, we were up there, on Mount Olympus.

DIONYSUS. (*Stentorian; exaggerated.*) And the cry rang out, "Who shall help this maiden?
Shall it be Herakles, he of legendary might?"

THALIA. "Or Pallas Athena, whose wisdom and cunning
Won the Trojan War."

DIONYSUS. "But NO, they turned to US:"

DIONYSUS & THALIA. "THE GODS OF COMEDY!" *Ta daaaa!*

DIONYSUS. How do you do. Dionysus. Later called Bacchus.

THALIA. Hi, I'm Thalia. Later called Thalia.

(*We hear a trumpet fanfare.*)

DAPHNE. Wow. You brought sound effects. That's just – please. Stay right where you are, I-I-I need to make one quick phone call –

THALIA. Aw, there's no need to be scared of us –

DAPHNE. *(Snatching something from the desk.)* Stay back! I can defend myself!

DIONYSUS. Death by stapler. Now that would be humiliating.

DAPHNE. Leave right this minute or I'll call the police!

DIONYSUS. I'm afraid the police can't help you at the moment.

> *(He snaps his fingers and we hear a police siren, then a screeching car collision, followed by the voices of angry police officers: "Hey, watch where you're goin'!" / "Are you nuts or somethin'?!" / "You coulda killed me!")*

THALIA. With tempers flarin' like that, we should cool 'em off, don't you think?

> *(She snaps her fingers and we hear thunder and it starts pouring rain outside. Then it starts snowing – inside the room, if possible.)*

DAPHNE. Snow?! Are you – …? What are you – …? *Ahhhhhhhhhhh!*

> *(She bolts away, runs this way and that and then runs under the desk. When she emerges out the other side, it's snowing on that side of the room, too.)*

AGH! *You're – you're crazy. These are tricks. Who are you really? Tell me. TELL ME!*

DIONYSUS. I'm sorry, kid.

> *(A scroll has now appeared in their hands and they unroll it with a snap. It reads*:)*

The Gods of Comedy

DIONYSUS & THALIA. *(Gently.)* We're the Gods of Comedy. *Ta daaaaa.*

---

* In the original production it was a banner that came down from the sky. Indeed, it could be anything legible and witty.

(A colorful little fireworks display goes off behind them.)

*(**DAPHNE** faints. Then Dixieland music* takes us into:)*

---

* A license to produce *The Gods of Comedy* does not include a performance license for any third-party or copyrighted music. Licensees should create an original composition or use music in the public domain. For further information, please see Music Use Note on page 3.

Scene Three

(A few minutes later. The room is empty, then
RALPH *and* **DEAN TRICKETT** *hurry on.)*

RALPH. Daphne? Daphne are you in there?

DEAN. Oh it's so tremendously exciting! And you're sure it's the entire play?

RALPH. It seemed complete.

DEAN. And the quality of the writing?

RALPH. You have no idea. It's better than *Alcestis* – or *Hippolytus.*

DEAN. Ha haaaaa! You know, every time I read the Greeks I think to myself, "That's it. That's the last of them." But now, thanks to you –

(She wipes a tear away.)

RALPH. I just kept at it.

DEAN. Exactly. That's what scholarship is. You don't give up, you keep looking and thinking. Now listen to me. As you know, this is Homecoming Weekend, and simply every one of our big donors will be here this year. I've heard that even Brooklyn DeWolfe is coming.

RALPH. The movie star?

DEAN. She was a student of mine. Sharp as a tack.

RALPH. She was in the *Tarzan* movies. She played Jane.

DEAN. Oh she did dozens of movies. And now she's doing television – the sidekick roles, I'm afraid – but my point is that we should seize the day and announce the book tonight while everyone's here.

RALPH. Tonight? I-I-Id like to spend a few days with it first.

DEAN. Of course, you would, but follow me closely. We have all the major donors here, tonight only, and they will simply swoon over this book of yours, it's the find of the century! And talk about Fate – the theme of the costume ball tonight is Greek Mythology. I plan to come as Artemis, Mistress of the Hunt!

RALPH. Well…it's all right with me.

DEAN. Excellent. Lets go find Daphne. Quickly. Wait!

> *(She poses.)*

> *"Polláh tah daynáh oodén ahn –*
> *thróhpoo daynoteron pélay."**

RALPH. "Many are the wonders of the world around us,
But nothing is more wonderful than the mind of Man."

DEAN. *Thank God for the Greeks!* Let's go!

> *(They exit, and the moment they're gone,*
> **DAPHNE** *and* **DIONYSUS** *hurry in from the*
> *other direction.)*

DAPHNE. Come on! Hurry up! We have to find it!

> *(**DIONYSUS** is wearing the latest in college*
> *fashion, eating a cheeseburger.)*

DIONYSUS. Holy Poseidon, this kingdom is *dazzling*! What
do you call it again?

DAPHNE. College.

DIONYSUS. Smoking, drinking, fornicating. Who invented
this place?

DAPHNE. I thought the ancient Greeks had universities.

DIONYSUS. Not like this they didn't. What's this thing called
again?

DAPHNE. A cheeseburger.

DIONYSUS. I should build a temple to it. "I bid you worship,
Holy Cheesebugger."

DAPHNE. Burger.

DIONYSUS. And your language is so colorful. What does
"badass" mean?

DAPHNE. Good.

DIONYSUS. "Sucks"?

DAPHNE. Bad.

DIONYSUS. "Phenom"?

---

* πολλὰ τὰ δεινὰ κοὐδὲν ἀν-
θρώπου δεινότερον πέλει·

DAPHNE. Star.

DIONYSUS. "Redonkulus"?

DAPHNE. Amazing. Would you stop this! I'm in trouble. You said you'd find the book.

DIONYSUS. All right, all right. Now we need a plan. We've got to be systematic about it. Admittedly, not my greatest virtue. So it's a book.

DAPHNE. Right. Only it's old and rare with loose pages and a red binding.

DIONYSUS. Let me ask you something.

DAPHNE. Shoot.

DIONYSUS. "Shoot"?

DAPHNE. It means tell me.

DIONYSUS. Ooh, I love that. Shoot me, baby. Draw that bow o' yours.

DAPHNE. Dionysus!

DIONYSUS. Sorry, sorry. But it's just a book. I mean, look around you. You've got sunshine. You've got burgercheeses. You need more fun in your life.

DAPHNE. Fun? I-I-I have plenty of fun.

DIONYSUS. Like what?

DAPHNE. I eat popcorn.

DIONYSUS. Oy vey.

DAPHNE. I cook.

DIONYSUS. What do you cook?

DAPHNE. Broccoli. Rice.

DIONYSUS. You're killing me here.

DAPHNE. It's healthy.

DIONYSUS. The gods are weeping.

DAPHNE. And I dance!

DIONYSUS. Don't tell me. The waltz.

DAPHNE. No, I *dance*.

DIONYSUS. Where?

DAPHNE. Alone.

DIONYSUS. *Where?*

DAPHNE. In my bedroom.

DIONYSUS. Are you naked?

DAPHNE. Stop it.

DIONYSUS. Do you take pictures?

DAPHNE. *Would you stop it!* The book I lost, it would change our understanding of the Ancient World. The role of Fate, the role of the gods, and if I don't find it he'll never speak to me again.

DIONYSUS. Who won't?

DAPHNE. Ralph.

DIONYSUS. Who's Ralph?

DAPHNE. He's a colleague of mine. He trusted me with it.

DIONYSUS. A "colleague"?

DAPHNE. Someone I work with.

DIONYSUS. I know what the word colleague means, but you have piqued my interest.

DAPHNE. I-I don't know what you mean.

DIONYSUS. Oh please. He's not just a colleague, now is he?

DAPHNE. Of course he is.

DIONYSUS. Is he your lover?

DAPHNE. No.

DIONYSUS. But you'd like him to be.

DAPHNE. I didn't say that.

DIONYSUS. But you get all badass when you see him. You think he's redonkulous.

> (**THALIA** *enters, also wearing a very college outfit. She looks marvelous in it. She, too, has soaked in the environment.*)

THALIA. Man, you gotta see this place. It is dope!

DIONYSUS. What are those?

THALIA. They're called French fries.

DIONYSUS. *(Trying a French fry.)* Zeus's balls! How do they make these things?

THALIA. They're potatoes.

DIONYSUS. You mean they grow like this? Can I get the seeds?

THALIA. They've also got this nectar made by somebody called Dr. Pepper.

DIONYSUS. Hey, listen, I discovered why she wants the book. She thinks she's in love.

THALIA. *(Sarcastic.)* No kidding, Kronos.

DIONYSUS. You knew this? How did you know this?

THALIA. It's always love. It's how things work down here. It's like talkin' to a cyclops.

> (**DAPHNE** *chokes back a sob.*)

Hey. You want to hear their school song? *(Aside to* **DIONYSUS.***)* It'll cheer her up. *(Aloud.)* I saw a bunch of 'em practicing it for the big game tomorrow.

DIONYSUS. Oh, right! I saw it, too!

> (*They sing the song. It's sung to the familiar tune of the 1908 Notre Dame University Victory March "fight song."* **DAPHNE** *watches them, looking miserable and does not join in.*)

DIONYSUS & THALIA.
GO SCORE A TOUCHDOWN TODAY,
WE'RE NOT AFRAID OF BATTLE OR FRAY.
WE CAN BEAT THE OTHER SIDE AND
TEAR 'EM TO PULP AND KICK THEIR HIDE.

GO SHOW 'EM WE'RE ON A QUEST,
WE'LL WIN THE GAME NO MATTER THE TEST.
WE CAN MAKE THEM CRY WITH PAIN
'CAUSE WE ARE THE COLLEGE BEST!

> (*They chant in rhythm.*)

DIONYSUS.
FIGHT FOR THE SCHOOL AND
SCORE THAT GOAL,

THALIA.
> BEAT THE OTHER FELLOW AND
> LOSE YOUR SOUL,

DIONYSUS.
> I'M NOT A JOCK,

THALIA.
> I'M FULL OF SASS,

DIONYSUS & THALIA.
> IT'S DOWN THE FIELD
> AND KICK THEIR OOOOOOOOOOOOH

> *(They pull* **DAPHNE** *into the final verse and she tries, lamely, to join their dance.)*

> WE'LL CLEAN THEIR CLOCKS TILL THEY LOSE,
> WE'LL BURN THEIR SOCKS AND THEIR SHOES,
> WE'VE NO SHAME, WE'LL WIN THE GAME
> 'CAUSE WE ARE THE COLLEGE BEST!

> *(Pow! Confetti! Lights! When it's over,* **DAPHNE** *weeps aloud.)*

DAPHNE. *Whaaaaa!*

DIONYSUS. Everybody's a critic.

DAPHNE. I'm so sorry. It's just that it's getting later and later and if I can't find the book I don't know *what* I'll do!

> *(She continues crying.)*

THALIA. Hey we'll find it, I promise.

DAPHNE. You *can't* promise! You *can't*! And it's all my *fault*!

> *(She is weeping openly now.)*

THALIA. Di, *(Sotto voce, indicating the scroll.)* she needs an adventure.

DIONYSUS. Adventure, adventure. We can do this. Wait! The Himalayas. You scale to the top.

THALIA. Your fingers are frozen.

DIONYSUS. Your nose falls off but you've made a difference!

DAPHNE. I don't like the cold.

DIONYSUS. Scuba diving.

THALIA. With the mask and goggles.

DAPHNE. I can't swim!

THALIA. Okay, a trip.

DIONYSUS. Maybe a singles' cruise. Where would she go?

THALIA. Disney World.

DIONYSUS. Ooh good idea. It's so happy there.

THALIA. With the costumes.

DIONYSUS. And mice.

THALIA. And songs.

DIONYSUS. And those incredible lyrics!

DIONYSUS & THALIA.
> IT'S A NICE WORLD AFTER ALL.
> IT'S A NICE WORLD AFTER ALL...

DAPHNE. *WHAA!*

DIONYSUS. *(To* **THALIA**.*)* Okay, let's work on the happy ending.

THALIA. Right. Daphne, sweetheart, what's the name of the play? If we're going to find it we'll need the title.

DAPHNE. It's called *Andromeda*. It's based on the story of Andromeda and

DIONYSUS & THALIA. Perseus.

> (**DIONYSUS** *and* **THALIA** *look at each other with a gleam of excitement.*)

DIONYSUS. Are you sure that's it?

DAPHNE. Of course I'm sure.

THALIA. Holy Helenus.

DAPHNE. What? What is it?

THALIA. *Andromeda* is Zeus's favorite play *ever*!

DIONYSUS. He saw it just once at the first performance –

THALIA. then Euripides died in Macadamia.

DIONYSUS. That's Macedonia. The play was lost

THALIA. and Zeus has always, *always* wanted to read it!

DIONYSUS. *Ha!* Ooh this could be good.

THALIA. He'd be so impressed.

DIONYSUS. And *grateful.*

    (They laugh gleefully and spring into action.)

THALIA. Right. Let's do this thing.

    (Shaking her hands out.)

I'll need some room.

DIONYSUS. Stand back.

    *(**THALIA** begins her heavy-breathing ritual. They take this ritual seriously. It is not slapstick.)*

DAPHNE. *(Whispering.)* What's she doing?

DIONYSUS. It's called meditation. It puts her into the past.

THALIA. *Shhh.*

DIONYSUS. Sorry.

DAPHNE. Sorry.

THALIA. *Mmmmmm.*

DIONYSUS. *(Joining **THALIA**.) Mmmmmm.*

DAPHNE. *(Joining both of them.) Mmmmmm.*

    *(The lights change. **THALIA** chants:)*

THALIA. *Explore the dark,*
   Run where you will,
   In nooks and corners
   Swift or still.
   Where mortal world
   Is left behind
   In shifting sands
   Of shifting time.
   Seek high and low,
   Seek everywhere
   With sight of lynx
   And might of bear.
   Then seek thy soul
   From sky to ground
   And tell us where

The past is found.
Mmmmmmm.

DIONYSUS & DAPHNE. *(Joining* **THALIA**.*) Mmmmmmm.*

(**THALIA** *is in a trance by this time.*)

THALIA. I see a book. It is here on this desk.

DAPHNE. She's right, that's where it was –

DIONYSUS. *Shhhh.*

THALIA. I see it falling into a basket. Here. The book is borne aloft in powerful hands that carry it to a machine.

(**DAPHNE** *gasps.*)

A page from the book is removed and fed to the monster.

(We hear the sound of the shredder: Grrrrrshunk!)

DAPHNE. Oh my God. No one would do that. It's impossible.

DIONYSUS. What is it?

DAPHNE. It's a *shredder*! It shreds paper into little shards of – *AGHHH! Look at this! It's some of the manuscript! Oh my God! OH MY GOD!*

THALIA. Calm down! Breathe!

DAPHNE. Who would do such a thing!

DIONYSUS. Wait! Look! There isn't much paper.

DAPHNE. Well where's the rest of it?

DIONYSUS. I have no idea.

DAPHNE. *(Shaking* **DIONYSUS**.*) WELL DO SOMETHING AND FIND IT!*

THALIA. *Apollo?*

DIONYSUS. *Apollo!*

DAPHNE. You're calling Apollo?

DIONYSUS & THALIA. *Apollo, Apollo, Apollo, Apollo –*

DAPHNE. But why Apollo?

DIONYSUS. He's the Great Healer.

THALIA. The God of Light.

DIONYSUS. And his Oracle at Delphi is the source of Truth.

THALIA. *Apollo, Apollo,*

DIONYSUS. *Apollo, Apollo,*

> (**DAPHNE** *joins in.*)

ALL THREE. *Apollo, Apollo –*

> *(Celestial noise.)*

THALIA. He's coming!

DIONYSUS. Stand back!

THALIA. He's here in all his glory!

> *(Celestial light, smoke and noise. Then bang, the door flies open and it is not Apollo. Instead, **ARES**, the God of War, strides into the room. Homer calls him the curse of mortals.)*

> *(He is large and unshaven, with bulging muscles. He wears battered armor and leather boots and has a blood-stained sword at his belt. He is rude, bellicose and tremendously manly.)*

ARES. *WHAT THE FUCINUS LACUS AM I DOING HERE?!*

THALIA. Oh no.

DIONYSUS. It's Ares.

DAPHNE. Ares?

THALIA. The God of War.

DIONYSUS. She made a mistake.

THALIA. I didn't make a mistake. You made a mistake.

DIONYSUS. I didn't make a mistake.

DAPHNE. *Well somebody made a mistake!*

ARES. *(Picking **DIONYSUS** off the ground and shaking him.) I SAID WHAT AM I DOING HERE?!*

DIONYSUS. Brother Ares, we-we need help for this lady who is in distress so we called upon your gracious oneness to come to her aid.

DAPHNE. Well in fact we called upon –

*(**DIONYSUS** and **THALIA** gestures "No!")*

you for more than just help, O God of War. For I find that I am sorely vexed and I need your might and strength and iron will to save me from an unjust fate.

ARES. You have chosen wisely, madam. Who do I kill?

DAPHNE. Kill?

ARES. Would you have me slaughter the Corinthian Boar that challenged Hercules on the Shores of Cadmus?

DAPHNE. Not quite.

ARES. Or defeat the dreaded man-eating Mares of King Diomedes? I will chop them to pieces.

DAPHNE. Well no. I mean... I lost a book.

ARES. What?

DAPHNE. A book.

ARES. You have summoned me here to find a book?!

DAPHNE. *(Standing up to him.)* Yes, it's a book. It's an important book!

ARES. *Do not provoke me, wretched headstrong girl, or in my immortal rage I will turn thy Spirit into clay and nothingness!*

THALIA. Hey, hey, she's just a kid.

DIONYSUS. You should cut her some slack.

THALIA. Slack?

DIONYSUS. It means give her a break.

THALIA. A break?

DIONYSUS. It means like backing off and being understanding –

ARES. WHAT ARE YOU TALKING ABOUT?! *(To* **DIONYSUS.***) You.* You have vexed me time and again and *I will make you pay for it*!!

DIONYSUS. Well that's insulting. How dare you, sir.

ARES. I challenge you to a duel to the death.

DIONYSUS. When?

ARES. Tomorrow at dawn.

DIONYSUS. Excellent!

(Knocks on **ARES**' *breastplate. Knock, knock!)*

Nice armor.

ARES. This is my chest.

DIONYSUS. What about the day after tomorrow?

ARES. *(Sniff. Sniff sniff.)* What land is this? It smells of mortal toil.

DIONYSUS. It is called College, Brutality, and is filled with unanticipated joys of the flesh.

ARES. Then I will go explore it. But do not leave this mortal pasture until I return. *(To* **DIONYSUS**.*) I HAVE NOT FINISHED WITH YOU!*

(He exits and they all breathe a sigh of relief.)

DIONYSUS. Whoa.

THALIA. That was close.

DAPHNE. How did I ever get myself into this? I don't even *like* adventures. I like love stories and happy endings. I like *I Love Lucy.*

DIONYSUS. *(As Ricky Ricardo.)* "Lucy, you got some 'splainin' to do."

THALIA. *(As Lucy Ricardo.)* "Whaaaa!"

DAPHNE. *(Crying.)* Whaaaa!

DIONYSUS. Hey, c'mon. It'll be all right.

THALIA. Yeah, what else could happen?

RALPH. *(Off, from below the window.) Daphne? Are you up there?*

DAPHNE. Oh no. It's him.

DIONYSUS. Him who? Who's him?

DAPHNE. It's Ralph! It's Ralph!

THALIA. *(At the window.)* Is that your boyfriend? Wow, he's cute.

DIONYSUS. Down, Pegasus.

DAPHNE. Where can I go? I don't want to see him!

DIONYSUS. Hide her in the closet.

THALIA. What about the shredder?

DAPHNE. The shredder?

DIONYSUS. Behind the shredder?

THALIA. What about the *paper*?

DIONYSUS. You mean under the paper?

DAPHNE. No, he'll see the paper.

DIONYSUS. Then hide the paper and put her in the closet.

THALIA. The closet?

DIONYSUS. What closet?

DAPHNE. *THERE IS NO CLOSET!*

RALPH. Daphne?

> *(As **RALPH** enters, **DIONYSUS** and **THALIA** snap their fingers.)*

DAPHNE. Ahh! Oh, Ralph! I-I-I've been looking for you. Now listen, I-I have something to tell you.

> *(**RALPH** walks right past her and calls into the alcove.)*

RALPH. Daphne? Are you in there? Daphne?

DAPHNE. What – ? What happened? Ralph? Ralph?

RALPH. *(Picks up the phone and hits two numbers.)* Hi Caroline? Is Dean Trickett there? I'm looking for Daphne. Sure, I'll hold.

DAPHNE. What's happening? Can't he –?

DIONYSUS & THALIA. Ha haaaaa!

DIONYSUS. We did it!

THALIA. It worked!

DAPHNE. Am I invisible?

THALIA. You got it, baby.

DIONYSUS. Not too shabby.

THALIA. "Shabby"?

DIONYSUS. Ratty or moth-eaten.

DAPHNE. But I can feel my arms! I-I-I have substance. And I can see both of you.

THALIA. You can snap to order. There's nothin' to it.

DIONYSUS. It's like being an artist. You want a tragedy?

(*Snap!*)

The King is dead.

THALIA. You want a comedy?

(*Snap!*)

The lovers meet.

DIONYSUS. Thriller.

(*Snap!*)

THALIA. Thrombosis.

(*Snap!*)

DIONYSUS. Bald.

(*Snap!*)

THALIA. Bereft.

(*Snap!*)

(*Every time* **THALIA** *or* **DIONYSUS** *snap their fingers, a different reality instantly sets in for* **RALPH**. *So above,* **RALPH** *is dying, in love, frightened, having a heart attack, grabs the back of his head, and feels bereft. This all happens very rapid-fire. Then we hear* **CAROLINE***'s voice through the phone:* "Hello? Hello?")

RALPH. What? Oh right, still here. Right, just have her call me back. Thanks.

(*He hangs up the phone, bemused.*)

DAPHNE. This is amazing.

THALIA. Yeah.

DAPHNE. Ha ha! Look at this. And this! And this!

(*She dances in front of* **RALPH**. *She shimmies. She's outrageous.*)

I'M INVISIBLE!!

THALIA. Except sometimes you see things you wish you hadn't.

DAPHNE. What do you mean?

BROOKLYN. Knock, knock.

> (**BROOKLYN DEWOLFE** *appears in the doorway. She is dressed to the nines.* **MISS DEWOLFE** *is a movie star with a smile that makes you believe in God. She is stunningly beautiful and tremendously stylish. Her makeup is perfect. Her dress is perfect. Her shoes are perfect. She is perfect.*)

Excuse me? Is this the Classics Department?

RALPH. Yes it is.

BROOKLYN. I'm looking for the head of the department, Professor Sargent.

RALPH. That's me.

BROOKLYN. No, really.

RALPH. Yes. Why not?

BROOKLYN. But you're so young. Sorry. I didn't mean to be rude. How do you do. I'm –

RALPH. Brooklyn DeWolfe. The movie star. I heard you were here and I couldn't believe it. It's great to meet you.

> *(They shake hands.)*

My gosh, that spy movie with Brad Pitt –

BROOKLYN. *Brothers in Arms*.

RALPH. You shook hands like this over a desk in Moscow.

BROOKLYN. My salad days when I was green in judgment. You know that I'm in awe of you.

RALPH. Me? I'm just a professor.

BROOKLYN. "Just a professor." I've read your writings on Greek mythology and oh my God, your *books*.

RALPH. I heard you were a terrific student here.

BROOKLYN. That's the Dean talking, I imagine. We have a mutual admiration society.

RALPH. Well I'm glad you're here.

BROOKLYN. So am I. Especially because of this find of yours. She just told me about it and oh my Lord, it's thrilling. When I was in Athens a few years ago filming something or other –

RALPH. *Cleopatra Returns*?

BROOKLYN. *Colon: The Revenge of the Coptics*. Well while I was there, we had a tour of this amazing museum that was filled with manuscripts –

RALPH. The Benaki.

BROOKLYN. Right. And I fell in love with them. I loved holding them, and feeling their history. Oh, I can't tell you how much I envy you, living a quiet life with all these books around you.

RALPH. I feel pretty lucky.

BROOKLYN. And now you've done this remarkable thing. *Andromeda*. What a story. Can you imagine when it's produced? It'll be a sensation.

RALPH. Produced?

BROOKLYN. Of course.

RALPH. I hadn't thought of that. We could do a student production.

BROOKLYN. A student production? Professor, you've got a bombshell here! Don't you realize? Think of the great productions of Greek drama over the past fifty years. Of *Elektra*. And *Antigone*. And *Oedipus Rex* with *Laurence Olivier*. Be still my heart, you're talking the National Theatre, Stratford, Broadway. And then there's the movie, of course. They'll just snap up the rights.

RALPH. You think so?

BROOKLYN. Well of course they will. It has adventure and romance and costumes and a monster. It's a Marvel comic book with class. It'll be a *sensation*. Just make sure you get the best studio and the best producer. That's the key.

RALPH. Will I have a say in all that?

BROOKLYN. Of course you will. You found it. Think of all the movies that are based on books like this. It's like *Troy. Spartacus. Game of Thrones*! And oh my God, what a part for the right actress. *Andromeda. Chained to a rock to save her country. The sea monster coming at any moment, its teeth bared, its tail lashing.*

> *(Playing Andromeda for all she's worth, her arms above her head as if her wrists are chained together.)*

"If the Gods allow, let the serpent have its way with me, let it rise up from the depths of the ocean and penetrate this cave of mine where I wait in defiance of its cruelty and wrath.

"But hear me, Gods in Heaven, hear me I beg you! Let my suffering mean something to this world of ours! Let it make a difference! Let it save my people!"

> *(Her eyes well up.)*

Sorry, it just…it moves me even when I think about it.

RALPH. Oh my gosh. I've got the best idea.

BROOKLYN. What's that?

RALPH. You should play it. Andromeda. You'd be fantastic.

BROOKLYN. Me?

DAPHNE. Ralph…

RALPH. Of course. You're perfect for it. You're beautiful and vulnerable and-and-and innocent. And you're a star! You could make everything happen!

BROOKLYN. Wow. I'm… I'm so surprised. And flattered.

RALPH. Would you do it?

BROOKLYN. Well, I'd have to talk with my agent, of course. I have other commitments –

RALPH. We'll just wait.

BROOKLYN. You will?

RALPH. Of course. I mean, you're perfect for this.

BROOKLYN. Golly, I never even thought about it… Oh!

(She gets something in her eye.)

Oh. Ow! Sorry. Oooh.

RALPH. Are you okay?

BROOKLYN. It's just these old books. It's all the dust. There's something in my eye. Oooh.

RALPH. Here, let me help. I'm good at this.

BROOKLYN. Really?

(She leans her head back and he pulls her eyelid open. Their faces are very close.)

RALPH. It's one of the few things I do pretty well.

BROOKLYN. "Few things."

(He examines her eye.)

RALPH. I don't see anything.

BROOKLYN. It feels like a tennis ball.

RALPH. I did consider a medical career.

BROOKLYN. So then we've lost one of the great physicians.

RALPH. Asclepius.

BROOKLYN. Gesundheit.

RALPH. Funny.

BROOKLYN. Thanks.

RALPH. Oh there it is. I think. It's pretty small. Let's try it.

(He puts the tip of his finger against her eye, then takes it away – but their faces stay close...and they kiss.)

DAPHNE. Ralph!

DIONYSUS. You slut!

RALPH. Oh my gosh. I'm sorry.

BROOKLYN. Oh don't be, please.

RALPH. I-I don't know how I could have –

BROOKLYN. Please. It's now the best reunion I ever went to. But you know I still haven't seen that book of yours.

RALPH. I know. I-I was about to look for it when you walked in.

BROOKLYN. "Look for it"?

RALPH. Right after I found it, I wanted to tell the Dean but I didn't want to carry it around, so I asked my assistant to keep an eye on it.

DAPHNE. "Assistant"? I'm your "*assistant*"?

RALPH. I don't know where she went. She probably took it to the library or something. She's very loyal.

BROOKLYN. Loyal?

DAPHNE. I sound like a dog.

BROOKLYN. She sounds like a dog!

(*They laugh together.*)

You don't mean old Mrs. Dumper who used to work here, do you? Greasy white hair –?

RALPH. No, no, her name's Daphne.

BROOKLYN. Daphne Dumper?

RALPH. (*Laughing.*) No, no. Her last name's Rain. And her hair is brown, but it's sort of limp.

BROOKLYN. She has a limp?

RALPH. No, her *hair* is limp.

(*They laugh.*)

BROOKLYN. Oh, she sounds a treat. Well. I should get to the reception. May I see the book later?

RALPH. Of course you may. Shall I walk you over?

BROOKLYN. Gee, I'd like that.

(*He takes her hand so she doesn't trip.*)

RALPH. Careful. Hold on. Too many books.

BROOKLYN. Oh you could never have too many books for me. I'm in love with books. I sleep with books.

RALPH. O happy books.

BROOKLYN. (*Laughing.*) Oh stop it!

(*They exit.* **DAPHNE** *is speechless.*)

DIONYSUS. You know sometimes people say things they don't even –

DAPHNE. "O happy books"?

THALIA. I wouldn't take it too much to –

DAPHNE. *Jesus Christ!*

> *(She turns on* **DIONYSUS** *and* **THALIA** *like a spitfire.)*

Now you listen to me. I want that *book* and I want it *now*! That is your *job*!

DIONYSUS. Okay, okay.

> *(They snap their fingers.)*

RALPH. *(Offstage.)* Brooklyn, wait a second, I forgot my keys.

BROOKLYN. *(Offstage.)* You got it! I'll meet you there!

> *(***RALPH*** *enters.)*

DAPHNE. Oh just look at him. Men are so smug, aren't they.

> *(***RALPH*** *looks up, startled. We realize that* **RALPH** *can see her, but* **DAPHNE** *doesn't realize it yet.)*

Do you realize that if Ralph finds out that I lost the book he'll never speak to me again?

THALIA. Daphne –

DIONYSUS. Daph –

DAPHNE. So I lost the book. It's not a federal crime.

DIONYSUS. Stop talking.

THALIA. Just stop!

DAPHNE. Why? What happened?

RALPH. You lost the book?

DAPHNE. Yes I lost the *AHHHHHHHH*! *Ralph!* I-I-I thought you couldn't even – ...He can hear me?!

DIONYSUS. We snapped. You didn't hear us snap?

THALIA. I guess we should have told ya.

DAPHNE. You should have "told me"?

RALPH. Who are you talking to? And what do you mean you lost the book? Our book?

DAPHNE. It's not that simple.

RALPH. Of course it is. You were holding the book. Did you lose the book?

DAPHNE. No, of course not!

RALPH. Oh thank God.

DAPHNE. I-I-I misplaced it. And then it went missing.

RALPH. The book is missing?

DAPHNE. Yes. No. I mean I just can't find it.

RALPH. Which means you lost it.

DAPHNE. No, I didn't *lose* it.

RALPH. Then you have the book?

DAPHNE. No I don't have the book.

RALPH. So you lost the book?

DAPHNE. *YES I LOST THE BOOK! ALL RIGHT?! I LOST IT! IT'S GONE! I LOST THE BOOK!*

RALPH. *(Fighting with himself like Jekyll and Hyde.)* But how could you – how could – *how could you lose it?! You just had to stand here and hold it for a minute. I mean how is it possible TO LOSE A BOOK WHEN YOU'RE HOLDING IT?!* GRK! GRK! GRK! I'm sorry, I'm sorry, I shouldn't get angry, and you must feel awful and I'm sure it's hard for you to tell me this when you *JUST HAD TO STAND HERE AND HOLD THE BOOK, IT'S INCREDIBLE!*

DAPHNE. I made a mistake, all right?! I'm sorry! Your *assistant* made a mistake!

DIONYSUS. And now it begins.

> *(They pull out some popcorn and watch as if at the movies.)*

DAPHNE. Of course an *assistant* can't be *trusted* with anything *important*, can she?

RALPH. Oh my God, were you *hiding* in here? How did you hear that? And I didn't mean you were an assistant, the word just-just-just popped out.

DAPHNE. Oh you were popping all right. "O happy books." You were popping out all over the place.

RALPH. She's a star, okay? I got carried away!

DAPHNE. *Is that why you kissed her?! Do you kiss every star who carries you away?*

RALPH. Where were you hiding?

DAPHNE. You have no idea.

DIONYSUS. You can tell him about us, you know.

THALIA. We don't mind in the least.

DAPHNE. He'll think I'm crazy.

THALIA. Not when he sees us.

DAPHNE. It'll scare him to death.

RALPH. Scare who to death?

DAPHNE. *I wasn't talking to you.*

> *(From this point on,* **RALPH** *gets worried about* **DAPHNE**. *He realizes that she's talking to imaginary friends and may be losing her mind.)*

THALIA. *(Eyeing* **RALPH**.*)* You could tell him about my trance if ya want. He might be impressed.

DAPHNE. Are you flirting with him?

THALIA. Well he's pretty cute.

DAPHNE. He's *not* cute. He thinks he's cute.

RALPH. Daphne, I-I-I think you should sit down for a minute.

DAPHNE. Oh, please. Let's skip this part. I'm not crazy. I'm not seeing little elves in the trees.

> *(***DIONYSUS** *and* **THALIA** *pose as little elves in trees to be funny.)*

I guess we should tell him.

THALIA. Yeah, let's do that. I'd like to meet him.

RALPH. Daphne, I'm going to make a call now.

DAPHNE. Oh just sit down for a minute. Or stand up. Oh, I don't care. How do I tell you this –? Ralph, I've been visited by an unearthly presence.

RALPH. Oh. I see.

DAPHNE. No you don't see! And don't be patronizing! Oh, how do I do this.

THALIA. We could fade into view.

DIONYSUS. Or make dog noises like Cerberus –

THALIA. and scare the pants off him! *Rower! Ruff! Ruff!*

DIONYSUS. *Mroooowwww!*

DAPHNE. Would you two stop it!

RALPH. Oh, Daphne, I'm really sorry. When you lost the book you must have gotten so upset. But your mental health is more important than a book –

DAPHNE. Ralph, stop talking. Now look this way. I want you to meet some visitors who arrived today. This is Dionysus, the God of Wine and Misrule, and this is his companion Thalia, the Muse of Comedy. This is Ralph Sargent. Now please appear.

> *(Beat. Nothing changes, but* **RALPH** *humors* **DAPHNE** *by pretending to see them and shaking hands with the air.)*

RALPH. Hello there. How do you do.

THALIA. Ha!

DIONYSUS. Poor kid, she must feel like an idiot.

DAPHNE. Of course I feel like an idiot! He thinks I'm insane! Now *do* something! Appear! Impress him!

DIONYSUS. Wait! I have an idea. Watch the flowers.

> *(***DIONYSUS** *picks up some flowers from a nearby bowl and moves them across the room – and* **RALPH**, *seeing only the moving objects, not* **DIONYSUS**, *freaks out.)*

RALPH. Ah!

THALIA. Oh good idea! The old dancing flowers.

> *(She takes some more and dances around the room with them.)*

RALPH. *Ahhhh!*

DIONYSUS. Shaking flowers.

THALIA. Skipping flowers.

DIONYSUS. Spinning flowers.

RALPH. *Ahh! Ahh!!* How are you doing this?!

DIONYSUS. And now it's time to come clean, my dear.

(We hear a drumroll.)

Countdown, please.

(Drumroll louder. And on each number, something else happens: books fly off the shelves, a picture falls, etc.)

THALIA. Starting at five!

DIONYSUS. Four!

THALIA. Three!

DIONYSUS. Two!

*(***THALIA*** and ***DIONYSUS*** appear to ***RALPH*** magnificently to the **brassy strains of a Broadway chorus line number***. Music. Lights. Confetti. Fireworks.)*

DIONYSUS & THALIA. *Ta da!*

*(They do a kick routine from a Broadway chorus. Then suddenly they have top hats and canes. ***RALPH*** freaks out.)*

RALPH. *(Over the music.) AGH! AGH! AGH! AGH!! What did you do?! Stop it! Stop it! It can't be! Stop it! No! Please!!*

*(As ***RALPH*** climbs on the furniture to get away and make it stop: Blackout. **Dixieland music***.)*

End of Act One

---

* A license to produce *The Gods of Comedy* does not include a performance license for any third-party or copyrighted music. Licensees should create an original composition or use music in the public domain. For further information, please see Music Use Note on page 3.

ACT II

*(Toward the end of the intermission, we hear an upbeat **rhythm and blues number***.)*

Scene One

(We're on the campus in the late afternoon and it's magically beautiful. There are lamp posts, a couple of paths, a bench or two and a beautiful tree. Because it's reunion weekend, there could be a banner or two announcing the festivities, and there are fairy lights in the trees to make it all the more festive later in the evening.)

(The party has started and in the distance we hear party chatter.)

*(After a beat, **DEAN TRICKETT** enters dressed as Artemis. With her is a stag on wheels.)*

DEAN. Good evening, alumni, good evening, donors, and I am thrilled to welcome you to our one hundred and thirty-third Homecoming Weekend! Hurrah! As most of you know, I'm Marjory Trickett, Dean of Humanities, but this of course is a costume party so you see me now as Artemis, Mistress of the Hunt! And this is my hind, my Ceryneian Hind, who moves faster than a speeding arrow...when he feels like it. But remember,

---

* A license to produce *The Gods of Comedy* does not include a performance license for any third-party or copyrighted music. Licensees should create an original composition or use music in the public domain. For further information, please see Music Use Note on page 3.

we are gods, so don't be surprised if my hind comes to life when you are least expecting it.

Now later this evening, I will have a surprise for you. A wondrous, shocking, remarkable surprise from Ancient Greece – a *manuscript*! But that's all I'll say. The announcement will come in just two hours, so be back in your seats at eight o'clock and I will see you then. Come, Pygmalion, let's go raise some money!

> (*As she exits,* **DAPHNE** *and* **DIONYSUS** *hurry in carrying a few items, followed by* **THALIA** *and* **RALPH**. **DIONYSUS** *and* **THALIA** *are back in their Greek clothing from Act I, Scene Two.* **RALPH** *is in shock.*)

DAPHNE. Okay, there's a lot to do, so let's set up. Table.

DIONYSUS. Check.

DAPHNE. Chair.

DIONYSUS. Check.

DAPHNE. Books.

DIONYSUS. Check. And we'll need some snacks so I brought

> (*From his backpack.*)

oreos, some beef jerky, and four cheesebloggers.

DAPHNE. Dionysus, we have less than two hours! (*To* **RALPH** *and* **THALIA**.) You two stay here. Di, come quick, we need a lexicon and I forgot my computer.

> (*They exit, leaving* **RALPH** *and* **THALIA**.)

RALPH. I... I can't get over it. I can't – I just – I can't – ...

THALIA. You're so cute when you're confused.

RALPH. I'm not confused, I'm out of body.

THALIA. Oooh, nice one.

RALPH. So you're not from the past.

THALIA. Of course not. That's silly. We live right now, just like you do.

RALPH. On Mount Olympus.

THALIA. Yeah. Which is way up there.

(Squints.)

It's hard to see.

RALPH. Catullus writes about a golden age when the gods still came to visit us.

THALIA. It never stopped. And we're down here more than you think. You just can't see us unless we want you to.

RALPH. And you're immortal.

THALIA. Yeah.

RALPH. You never die.

THALIA. Nope.

RALPH. So like 2,000 years ago you knew Julius Caesar.

THALIA. Pain in the butt. Do this, do that.

RALPH. Alexander?

THALIA. He was not so great.

RALPH. John Lennon.

THALIA.

HE LOVED ME, YEAH, YEAH, YEAH.

I don't know why it seems so crazy to you. You write about us all the time. Isn't that your specialty?

RALPH. Well that's true. Except we think of you as mythical. Made up by the Greeks to explain misfortune. If the crops were bad, it was the Sun God's fault. If a child got sick, Apollo was unhappy.

THALIA. Wow, that's so interesting.

RALPH. Is it right?

THALIA. No, it's totally wrong. Misfortune happens all the time and sometimes we start it, sometimes you do.

RALPH. That's what Homer says in *The Odyssey*, in Book One.

THALIA. Who's Homer?

RALPH. You don't read Homer?

THALIA. No.

RALPH. Do you read any of the books that have been written about you? *The Iliad*? *The Metamorphoses*?

THALIA. Well reading isn't my best thing. The letters get kinda smooshed up together.

RALPH. I noticed that you squint a lot.

THALIA. I don't know why.

> (**RALPH** *thinks for a beat, then takes off his glasses and offers them to* **THALIA.**)

RALPH. Try these on.

THALIA. *(Suspicious.)* What are they again?

RALPH. They're called glasses.

THALIA. Oh yeah.

> (*Cautiously, she tries them on. They look great on her: strong dark frames on her petite face. They're a fashion statement; and she's thunderstruck by the sudden change in her vision.*)

Holy Saturn! I can see everything! Give me that!

> (*She grabs a book from the table –* The Odyssey *– and starts reading rapid-fire.*)

"'Ah my queen,' Odysseus the man of craft assured her, 'ravage no more your lovely face with tears or consume your heart with grieving –'" *Athena's backside! You're wonderful!*

> (*She throws her arms around his neck and kisses him. As she does,* **DAPHNE** *and* **DIONYSUS** *return.* **DAPHNE** *sees them kissing and is unfazed.*)

DAPHNE. Here he goes again. He's a big kisser.

RALPH. Hey, I didn't do anything!

THALIA. Di, Daphne, look at this! I can see everything! Ha haaaaa!

DAPHNE. That's great, but listen. The announcement is now in less than two hours and the Dean has invited CNN and the History Channel.

RALPH. Oh no. We're dead.

THALIA. We're kaput.

DIONYSUS. No we're not kaput.

DAPHNE. We have a plan.

RALPH. *(Derisively.)* A plan.

DAPHNE. What's the matter? Are you afraid of upsetting your new girlfriend Brooklyn?

RALPH. She's not my girlfriend.

DAPHNE. *(Imitating **BROOKLYN**.)* "I love books." "I sleep with books."

RALPH. That is so unfair.

DAPHNE. She's a snake.

RALPH. She's smart!

DAPHNE. *She's a phoney-baloney and you know it!*

DIONYSUS. Children, children. Daddy's watching. Now we have to get started!

THALIA. So what's the plan?

DIONYSUS. We write the play.

THALIA. The play by Euripides?

DIONYSUS. No, no. We write a play about Andromeda in the *style* of Euripides.

RALPH. I don't understand.

DIONYSUS. Look, all we need is a book that looks and sounds like the play she lost.

DAPHNE. Which we'll find.

DIONYSUS. But not in time for tonight. Tonight, we need something like the real play in case anybody wants to read a few lines at announcement time.

RALPH. But what if we never find the real one?

DIONYSUS. *I don't know.* I'm not an Oracle. But if we don't have anything soon you'll look like nincompoops, the college will be ridiculed, you'll lose your jobs and you'll probably never work again. Now you only have ninety-eight minutes left and by the way, I love this watch.

(And he is indeed wearing a watch.)

RALPH. *(To **DAPHNE**.)* Daphne, are you okay with all this?

DAPHNE. Hey, I've spent twenty-five years being the nicest girl in the room and I'm sick of it. Now Dionysus and I will do the writing while you two help with the binding.

THALIA. What do you mean?

DAPHNE. It has to *look* like it's a thousand years old –

DIONYSUS. and we can do it if we have the paper.

DAPHNE. *(To **THALIA**.)* So you and Ralph have to steal a very old book from the vault in the library. We have one there from the fourteenth century.

RALPH. But I can't get into the vault. It's access-restricted to librarians and Deans.

DIONYSUS. Aha. The kid's thinkin'. Which is why Thalia goes in as the Dean.

RALPH. But she's not a Dean.

DIONYSUS. Not *a* Dean. *The* Dean. Dean Trickett.

RALPH. But she doesn't even look like Dean Trickett.

DIONYSUS. Oh ye of little faith.

THALIA. Metamorphosis.

RALPH. But that's not real. Is it?

THALIA. You just *talked* about it. Ovid's *The Metamorphoses*. It's like a hundred stories about gods who change their shape, and what'dya think, it's all made up?

RALPH. Well, yes, I did. I-I –

THALIA. Mortals.

DIONYSUS. I don't know how they feed themselves.

THALIA. Okay, look at me. Now I'm Thalia, the Muse of Comedy with the beautiful hair and nails –

> *(She walks behind a tree and emerges instantly as **DEAN TRICKETT** in her Artemis costume – still wearing **RALPH**'s glasses.)*

> *(And of course the role is played by the actress playing **DEAN TRICKETT**.)*

(Note: whenever **THALIA-AS-THE-DEAN** *appears, she takes on the mannerisms and accent of* **THALIA**, *even though she's played by the actress who plays the* **DEAN**.*)*

THALIA-AS-THE-DEAN. and now I look like Dean Trickett but I'm really Thalia *without* the beautiful hair and nails.

(Looks at her nails.)

Ugh. What a mess.

DAPHNE. Holy Hannah.

RALPH. Can you change into anything?

THALIA-AS-THE-DEAN. Yeah, pretty much. Animals. Trees. I once turned into Sigmund Freud and then I got an Oedipal complex and *that* was confusing.

DAPHNE. Hey, come on! We have to get moving! Now go get the book!

THALIA-AS-THE-DEAN. You got it, kiddo. Hey, Ralph. Try and catch me! Ha haaaaaaaaa!

(She laughs hysterically and runs off, followed by a bewildered **RALPH**.*)*

(Meanwhile, **DAPHNE** *and* **DIONYSUS** *start setting up the table and computer.)*

DAPHNE. Do you type?

DIONYSUS. I learned on one of my last trips. It was 1930 and F. Scott taught me.

DAPHNE. F. Scott Fitzgerald?

DIONYSUS. He was writing *Gatsby* and I helped him punctuate. I told him we should have shared credit, but Zelda objected. She was a hellion. She wanted to sleep with Picasso but he refused because she only had one nose. Then of course she shacked up with Eleanor Roosevelt –

DAPHNE. *Dionysus, we're in a hurry!* Now I'll dictate, you type.

DIONYSUS. Whoa, whoa, whoa. *You'll* dictate? *I'll* dictate. I *knew* Euripides.

DAPHNE. That doesn't mean you can write like him.

DIONYSUS. What are you talking about? I'm a great writer. I told you, I worked with F. Scott Fitzgerald.

DAPHNE. I've been writing all my life.

DIONYSUS. In Greek? I've been writing in Greek.

DAPHNE. You just don't strike me as a very good writer.

DIONYSUS. I'm a god! Okay, fine. We'll do a test. First few lines in English, then we'll translate.

DAPHNE. Fine.

DIONYSUS. Fine!

> (As **DAPHNE** *pulls out her laptop,* **DIONYSUS** *sits at the table and pulls out his typewriter.*)

DAPHNE. What's that?

DIONYSUS. A 1926 Smith Corona Red Duotone portable with front-strike keys, a four-bank keyboard, wooden platen and auto-shift carriage displacement.

DAPHNE. I meant where did you get it?

DIONYSUS. Hemingway. Birthday present. You've got twenty-five seconds. On your mark, get set, go!

> (*They type. We hear the two different clickety-clacks of their machines, she on her computer, he on his Smith Corona. They're both absorbed. After several seconds of intense writing, they stop.*)

Okay, stop. Let's hear. You first.

DAPHNE. (*Reading from the screen.*) "Scene One. A cave near the sea. Andromeda and the Nurse. The Nurse speaks first:

'How I wish the air had never stirred, and the Wind
Had not taken your mother's boastings up to the Gods,
For in their anger, they sent a plague and made our plowings fallow

And our flowers dust, and now, to save our country,
You must be sacrificed to this savage creature of the Sea.'"

Your turn.

DIONYSUS. *(Reads.)* "Andromeda, buck naked. 'Woe is me. O woe. My woe is great. O woe. The woeful monster comes. It is full of woe,'" okay, okay, you write it!

(He puts fresh paper in the roller.)

Five thousand years old, I get no respect. I'll type. Start over.

*(**DIONYSUS** types away on his Smith Corona – clickety-clackety.)*

*(**Dixieland music***. Cross-fade to another part of campus where:)*

---

* A license to produce *The Gods of Comedy* does not include a performance license for any third-party or copyrighted music. Licensees should create an original composition or use music in the public domain. For further information, please see Music Use Note on page 3.

Scene Two

(**BROOKLYN** *is on a cell phone in the middle of a call. She's in costume for the party, dressed as Aphrodite, looking even more gorgeous and voluptuous than ever. We hear the sounds of the reception in the background.*)

BROOKLYN. Morris! Oh, don't apologize you worm, just listen. You're my agent. You should be here. *Now.* Because it's going to be the hottest property since *The Ten Commandments* and it's a female lead and she doesn't have to be twenty-two years old. And this professor-type nearly had an orgasm trying to get me to agree, but now we've got to nail it down and get it *signed.*

(*Nearby we see* **ARES** *putting champagne glasses on his shield so he can take them away and drink them.*)

You. Waiter. Come over here. Bring me a martini.

ARES. What is martini?

BROOKLYN. Don't be cute. Straight up with a twist.

ARES. What is twist?

BROOKLYN. Listen, fly boy. I've had a long day. My feet hurt, my agent is AWOL, and this morning I fell off my Nordic Track Linear Motion Elliptical Cross-Trainer so get me a drink or I'll scratch your eyes out!

ARES. *You do not speak to a god this way or you will live to regret it!*

(*He takes her phone, throws it on the ground and jumps up and down on it. She gasps and goes nuts, as only the loss of a cell phone can do to a mortal.*)

BROOKLYN. Are you crazy?! If this thing's broken, you're paying for it, *do you understand me*?!

(They glare at each other. Then she feels his muscle.)

BROOKLYN. ...Are you with anybody?

(Dixieland music; and the scene cross-fades to **DAPHNE** and **DIONYSUS** hard at work.)*

---

* A license to produce *The Gods of Comedy* does not include a performance license for any third-party or copyrighted music. Licensees should create an original composition or use music in the public domain. For further information, please see Music Use Note on page 3.

Scene Three

(Clackety-clackety. **DAPHNE** *is making up the play as* **DIONYSUS** *types. They're really flying now.)*

DAPHNE. "Andromeda, Daughter of Light and Remembrance, –"

DIONYSUS. Slow down, slow down! I can't keep up –

DAPHNE. Oh just move over, I can type it faster.

DIONYSUS. But my fingers fly like the wind.

DAPHNE. Just move!

(They change places and **DAPHNE** *starts typing like mad.)*

Oh I love writing. Is this what being a god feels like?

DIONYSUS. Not exactly. We don't create, we unleash.

DAPHNE. Unleash what?

DIONYSUS. The will to create. I don't know why. When mortals are with us, they start dreaming and then they get wild and passionate and they want to explode.

DAPHNE. *(Typing and writing.)* "No child should have to sacrifice herself to the gods, and now my thoughts dwell on happier times," oooh, that's good, it's really good – "and then," ha ha!, oh wait for it, "Then suddenly out of the sky comes Perseus, and he cries, 'Oh maiden of the Cave, do not despair, I see thee on the rock and I come to save thee!'"

DIONYSUS. Ha ha! Atta girl! Keep it up!

*(**DIONYSUS** massages her shoulders to keep her going and* **DAPHNE** *finds it pleasurable and lolls her head back and kisses his cheek and continues typing.* **DIONYSUS** *realizes what just happened and faces forward in shock.)*

DIONYSUS. Uh oh. Back to work. Just keep typing.

(Dixieland music*; and the scene cross-fades to:)

---

* A license to produce *The Gods of Comedy* does not include a performance license for any third-party or copyrighted music. Licensees should create an original composition or use music in the public domain. For further information, please see Music Use Note on page 3.

Scene Four

> (**BROOKLYN** *and* **ARES**, *making out against a tree. Really going at it. We hear the party in the background again.*)

BROOKLYN. Would you slow down, it's not a war!

> (*Ring!* **BROOKLYN**'s *phone rings and she pulls it out.*)

You're lucky this thing still works. (*Into the phone, annoyed.*) Yes, Morris, are you here yet? Oh for God's sake, it's not Nepal. Did you take Exit 12? Good, now look for a crowd of Greek gods. I'm dressed as Venus. No, not the Venus de Milo, you idiot. I have arms. (*To* **ARES**.) Don't go away.

> (*As she exits,* **DEAN TRICKETT** *enters.*)

DEAN. (*Calling.*) Ralph! Daphne! I need the book!

> (*She sees* **ARES**.)

Oh how do you do. That is quite a costume. Are you Herakles or a Titan?

ARES. I am Ares, son of Zeus and Hera, slayer of the Trojans and the God of War.

DEAN. Of course you are. Now I don't think we've met. I'm Marjory Trickett, Dean of Humanities. Or should I say Artemis, Goddess of the Hunt!

ARES. You are not Artemis. She is my sister and the God Apollo's twin.

DEAN. You sly boots, you, you know your Greeks. And you're an alumnus, I presume. Eh? Heh, heh. And what do you do for a living?

ARES. Rape and pillage.

DEAN. Ah, you're in banking. How wonderful! And you've obviously done well for yourself. This armor appears to be real gold.

ARES. Of course it is gold. My wealth is legendary.

DEAN. Really? Well, we must get acquainted. I'm chairing the Development Committee. Do you have a family?

ARES. Yes.

DEAN. Children?

ARES. Forty-six.

DEAN. Forty-six children? From how many wives?

ARES. Forty-six.

DEAN. Good God. Oh, now wait a second. You're pulling my leg, aren't you?

ARES. That is the custom here?

DEAN. Well it is, rather. It's a college campus.

ARES. And do you like having your leg pulled?

DEAN. *(Laughing happily.)* Yes, as a matter of fact I do.

ARES. All right, if you say so.

> *(He grabs her and turns her upside down and starts pulling her leg.)*

DEAN. *AGH! STOP IT! IT'S AN EXPRESSION!*

> *(He stops.)*

ARES. Where is other woman? She is not so confusing.

DEAN. Brooklyn? I think she went – ...Oh no, no, no. Don't you touch her. She is a very good donor and I don't want to offend her in any capacity.

ARES. I will find her.

DEAN. I said leave her *alone.*

ARES. *I WILL DO AS I PLEASE, I AM THE GOD OF WAR AND YOU WILL NOT INTERFERE OR I WILL RAIN DOWN THE VENGEANCE OF THE SKY UPON YOU!* Waiter!

> *(He exits.)*

DEAN. Banking can do terrible things to a person.

> *(As the **DEAN** exits, **RALPH** runs in carrying the book from the vault. He's in high spirits.)*

RALPH. We did it, we did it! We got the book from the vault! Ha ha! Thalia, come on, What are you waiting for? ...Thalia?

> (**THALIA**, *still in her guise as the* **DEAN** *and still wearing* **RALPH**'s *glasses, runs in, panting heavily.*)

THALIA-AS-THE-DEAN. I'm comin'. *(Pant, pant.)* Hoo! That Dean o' yours has gotta get some exercise. But we got the book!

RALPH. Right. And Dionysus is going to use the paper from *this* book – ...

THALIA-AS-THE-DEAN. To make the *other* book. *Andromeda.* He's gonna scrape the old writing off the pages, and write the *new* play where the *old* play was.

RALPH. So he's making a palimpsest.

THALIA-AS-THE-DEAN. A what?

RALPH. A palimpsest. It's been done for centuries. Nowadays we use x-rays to see both writings simultaneously.

THALIA-AS-THE-DEAN. Do you know everything?

RALPH. Almost nothing, apparently.

> *(We hear a voice, off, friendly but insistent.)*

VOICE. Hello! Sargent! Is that you?

RALPH. Oh no, it's the President of the college.

VOICE. Come meet some people. They're donors. You'll like 'em.

RALPH. Here. You hold the book, I'll be right back.

> *(As she takes the book, she impulsively kisses him on the lips.)*

Thalia...

VOICE. Sargent?

RALPH. *Coming, sir.* To be continued.

> *(He hurries off.)*

THALIA-AS-THE-DEAN. *(To the audience.)* "To be continued." Isn't he cute? I mean, you gotta hand it to these mortals. They know the train is comin' down the tracks and soon it's gonna be whamo bamo, but they keep striving and pushing and doin' their best. I mean penicillin, come on, good job. They're kinda like human palimpsests, ya know what I mean? They've got layers and layers, and there's so much stuff goin' on underneath that sometimes the other guy's gotta work hard to find it. And I guess that's the moral of this whole story. You gotta take a chance on yourself – and on the person who's sitting next to you – 'cause what's underneath just might surprise you.

DEAN. *(Offstage.)* Hello? Who is that over there? That costume you're wearing, it looks just like mine*!

THALIA-AS-THE-DEAN. Oh my gosh, it's the Dean. I gotta go.

> *(She hurries out – and* **RALPH** *hurries in, looking for* **THALIA**.*)*

RALPH. *(Entering, calling to an unseen guest.)* Thank you, sir. I'll see you again soon. Goodbye. It was nice to meet you.

> *(He looks around.)*

Thalia? Thalia, where are you?

> *(***DEAN TRICKETT** *enters. The real* **DEAN TRICKETT**. *No book, no glasses. She's still wearing her Artemis costume, of course.* **RALPH** *thinks it's* **THALIA**.*)*

> *(Note: she should enter from a different direction than the one where* **THALIA** *last exited.)*

Oh there you are. I couldn't find you. Wait. Before you say anything else.

> *(He kisses her on the mouth.)*

DEAN. ...Thank you.

RALPH. But how can it ever work out between us? You're a goddess. You're divine.

---

* The effect is done with a recording.

DEAN. *(Pleased, modest.)* Professor…

RALPH. And underneath that costume of yours, your body is amazing. It's like a heat-seeking missile.

DEAN. *(Looking down at her body.)* It is?

RALPH. You're the sexiest creature I've ever met. But what good is sex if we can't have a future together. You're immortal. You're going to live forever.

DEAN. I've only written two books.

RALPH. Do you know what I see when I look in your eyes?

DEAN. Cataracts?

RALPH. I see thousands of years of… Hey wait a second. Where's the book?

DEAN. Exactly. Now you said Daphne had it, and we're in a hurry.

RALPH. Not that book, the other book. The one with the pages.

DEAN. All books have pages.

RALPH. For the palimpsest.

DEAN. It's a palimpsest?

RALPH. No, we're making one.

DEAN. Out of what?

RALPH. The book.

DEAN. What book?

RALPH. *The one with the pages!* Look, I'm asking for the book that I handed to you a minute ago. We raided the library, nobody caught us, and you were wearing my glasses by the way and they happen to look very good on you*aaaaaaaaaa!* Oh my God! You're Dean Trickett! Of course you are. You're the Dean. Ha ha! You're my boss, and I'm just so stupid! *Grk! Grk! Grk!* Look, I've got to run. Great party. Big hit. Keep up the good work. I'll see you later. *Nyaaaaa!*

       (**RALPH** *runs off.*)

DEAN. When I throw a party, *I throw a party.*

*(We hear **Dixieland music*** and we cross-fade to:)*

Scene Five

(**DAPHNE** *and* **DIONYSUS** *are working on the
play.* **DAPHNE** *is typing. They're both worked
up with the excitement of creation – and the
pace and tone of the scene are red hot.)*

DIONYSUS. We're close to the end!

DAPHNE. Oh Lord Apollo, I love this.

DIONYSUS. All right, the monster's dead and the chains are
broken.

DAPHNE. And Perseus and Andromeda are alone. So what
does she say?

DIONYSUS. She says, she says –

DAPHNE. "My days on earth were not complete – were not
Fulfilled until at last your hand reached out
And touched my cheek."

DIONYSUS. Oooh, that's good! Keep going, keep going.
Think of Andromeda when the monster comes. He
needs a name. We'll call him Fred. Fred the Monster.
Ooh, that's good. She sees him and cries, "Woe. O woe
is me!" I hope you're getting this. "Get back you slimy
beast!" Then Perseus appears in the sky. He's wearing
those sandals with the little wings. "I come from the
heavens, heavens, heavens, heavens! To save you, save
you, save you, save you!" And down he swoops to fight
the filthy beast of Death. "Take *that* and *that* and now
some of *that, you beast*!" And he plunges his sword into
Fred's neck and he dies in agony! "Gyyyyaaaaaaaaaaa!"
Fred, not Perseus. *"Gryyyyaaaaaaaa! Glug."*

DAPHNE. Done.

(**DAPHNE** *jumps ups and pulls the paper from
the typewriter. She has used carbons so they
both have copies of what she's written. She
hands him one.)*

Here, let's read it. See what you think. You read Perseus.

(They read the typescript – and they read it with absolute passion – the passion of Romeo and Juliet at the height of their discovery and ecstasy. The scene gets hotter and hotter and their sexual temperatures get higher and higher as they throw themselves into it. By the end, **DAPHNE***'s final cry of "Perseus!" is sheer orgasm.)*

"My days on earth were not complete, were not
Fulfilled until at last your hand reached out
And touched my cheek."

DIONYSUS. "I raced through time and spirit to unite our souls.
And though I hold you now, your head is filled
With nightmares of the beast,"

DAPHNE. "O when it first appeared, my blood was cold,
And in my fear, I looked to heaven,"

DIONYSUS. "and there
You saw a speck on the sun, a puzzlement,"

DAPHNE. "And then it grew and came to life."

DIONYSUS. "And from high above, I heard your voice,
And I sprang to action,"

DAPHNE. "And you came!"

DIONYSUS. *"I did!"*

DAPHNE. *(Rising to a pitch of excitement.)* "And then I cried
out to the Sun itself: 'O Chariot
Of the Sky, I beg you to hasten and race
To the West and bring me NIGHT and BED and LOVE,
O bring me PERSEUS!'"

(And she grabs him and kisses him passionately.)

DIONYSUS. No. No, no. Bad idea. I would take advantage
of you.

DAPHNE. *(Kissing his neck and his chest.)* Take advantage.

DIONYSUS. Stop it!

DAPHNE. I can't help myself.

DIONYSUS. Of course not, I'm a god.

DAPHNE. Ohhhhh...

DIONYSUS. Look, you're very attractive. You're-you're-you're a flower –

DAPHNE. Then pluck me. Please! I want a life! I want experience! And not only that, it's in your instructions.

DIONYSUS. How do you know?

DAPHNE. Because I have the scroll.

> *(She pulls out the scroll.* **DIONYSUS** *is shocked. He feels his pockets.)*

DIONYSUS. Hey, give that back!

DAPHNE. It says right here: "She needs an *adventure* and a *happy ending.*"

DIONYSUS. *(Tussling for it.)* Would you just – just –

DAPHNE. Don't you understand, I'm made of marble and I want to live! *So carve* me. *Chisel* me. *Take me this instant and make something new!*

> *(She lets her blouse down from her shoulders, and from the back she looks like a nude Greek statue in marble. From the front, which only* **DIONYSUS** *can see, she's naked.)*

DIONYSUS. *NO! Put that back on, young lady!* You need some serious help.

DAPHNE. *(Desperate.)* I *do* need help. I am so stressed out!

> *(She cries.)*

DIONYSUS. Stressed out?

DAPHNE. "Full of anxiety, nervous, uneasy."

> *(They look at each other...and her tears stop and they both burst into laughter. All the anxiety and stress about the book and* **DAPHNE**'s *identity are released, and they scream with laughter.* **DIONYSUS** *imitates* **DAPHNE** *flashing him –.)*

DIONYSUS. Whoop!

(*And they laugh all the harder. Then:*)

DAPHNE. It's not funny! You were supposed to help me find the play and I don't even know how I lost it! I mean I was sitting there reading *Medea*, then Aleksi came in, we chatted for a minute, he said he'd come back and I went downstairs and then Aleksi – ...

(*Suddenly she sees the light and gasps.*)

Aleksi. That's it. Yes! Yes! That's it! I need his phone number! I'll be right back! Oh *Aleksi*!

(*She runs off.*)

(*At which moment,* **THALIA** *hurries in.*)

(*She looks like* **THALIA** *again – and she's not, of course, wearing the* **DEAN**'s *costume. She's back in her Greek clothes, and she's wearing her glasses and carries the book from the vault.*)

THALIA. Di.

DIONYSUS. Thalia! Quick!

THALIA. What is it?

DIONYSUS. It's Daphne! She's going off the rails. She took off her *blouse*.

THALIA. Di, that always happens. It's what we do. We're like *Spring Awakening*.

DIONYSUS. I know, but she's just so innocent and-and-and vulnerable.

THALIA. Yeah, Ralph is like that. Only I'm keepin' him.

DIONYSUS. Oh you are not. You always say that.

THALIA. I am!

DIONYSUS. You're not. He's mortal.

THALIA. So what? I could be mortal.

DIONYSUS. Oh sure. That would last about ten minutes. "My nails, my nails!"

THALIA. Okay, okay. I get distracted. But it's so unfair. You don't see Athena fallin' for mortals.

DIONYSUS. She's the Goddess of Wisdom. Comedy is love.

THALIA. And Wisdom is tough.

DIONYSUS. Comedy's a breeze.

THALIA. And Wisdom is storm.

DIONYSUS. Comedy is light.

THALIA. And Wisdom is shadow.

DIONYSUS. Comedy is friendship.

THALIA. And Wisdom is too.

DIONYSUS. Embrace me.

> *(They do.)*

All right, let's buck up, kid, we have a job to do.

THALIA. The book.

DIONYSUS. The book. *Except*, it sounds like she's got a lead on the book. So now we need to get her back with Ralph, and then we'll have

DIONYSUS & THALIA. the happy ending!

BROOKLYN. *(Offstage.) Are you insane!*

THALIA. It's Brooklyn!

ARES. *(Offstage.) I will call down the gods and your crops shall whither!*

DIONYSUS. And that's Ares, and he wants to kill me. Quick, hide.

> *(**DIONYSUS** and **THALIA** run behind a bush and look over it to spy on what happens – at which moment, **BROOKLYN** stalks in, followed by **ARES**.)*

BROOKLYN. I told you, I have to find my agent.

ARES. No.

BROOKLYN. Yes.

ARES. I order you to stay!

BROOKLYN. You "order" me? Because I'm a woman?

ARES. Because I am a god!

BROOKLYN. You see this is the problem with men. You guys strut around, beating your chest like King Kong, and we're supposed to be impressed with you? Get a grip.

(**ARES** *bellows and gestures boldly to the sky, and there is a sudden, frightening crack of thunder.*)

Oh, please. You think coincidence is going to impress me?

(*She walks off giving him the bird.* **ARES** *gives a cry of fury and follows her off.*)

DIONYSUS. I wish I could do that.

(**DIONYSUS** *makes the same gesture to the sky as* **ARES** *did, and we hear a "Boing!" from the sky instead.*)

THALIA. I think it takes practice. Wait! Somebody else is comin'!

(*They hide again and* **RALPH** *strides in being chased by* **DAPHNE.**)

DAPHNE. Would you just listen!

RALPH. No.

DAPHNE. It's important!

RALPH. *Don't you understand? I kissed the Dean. She thinks I'm insane.*

DAPHNE. Ralph! I think I found the manuscript.

RALPH. You found it?

DAPHNE. I think Aleksi has it. I think he took it thinking it was trash, and from what I saw in the office, he might not have shredded the whole thing.

RALPH. "Shredded"?

DAPHNE. And he's on campus! You see, I called his house and they said he was on his way to the bonfire to cheer on the football team for the big...

RALPH. "Bonfire"?

(*They look at each other.*)

DAPHNE & RALPH. *YAHHHHHH!*

> *(They run off and* **DIONYSUS** *and* **THALIA** *reemerge.)*

DIONYSUS. Bonfire...

THALIA. Are we sunk, do ya think?

DIONYSUS. No. Not if we get Ralph and Daphne together again. We can still have a happy ending.

THALIA. Right! But how do we do it?

DIONYSUS. Jealousy. You saw what happened in the office. We just need Brooklyn.

THALIA. Well that part's easy. Change into Brooklyn.

DIONYSUS. Me?

THALIA. Yeah. I played the Dean so now it's your turn.

DIONYSUS. Oh, great.

THALIA. And hurry up. I'll bring Ralph and Daphne back!

> *(As she runs off,* **DIONYSUS** *calls after her.)*

DIONYSUS. But I'm lousy as a woman! I don't have the walk! ... "Change into Brooklyn." Okay, here goes nothin'.

> *(***DIONYSUS*** walks behind the tree, then reemerges looking like* **BROOKLYN** *in all her beauty. She is played of course by the actress playing* **BROOKLYN.** **DIONYSUS** *was right, he doesn't do well as a woman. He teeters on his high heels and doesn't know how to shift all the moving parts.)*

DIONYSUS-AS-BROOKLYN. Just look at me. The shoes don't fit, the heels are murder, and who the hell invented Spanx!

> *(He pulls out a pocket mirror.)*

Oh. Oh! Well. Not so bad.

> *(He sings as Ado Annie in* Oklahoma!, – *and he sings wonderfully like a musical comedy star.)*

I'M JIST A GIRL WHO CAIN'T SAY NO,
I'M IN A TURRIBLE FIX.

(He feels his throat. Where did that come from?)

With this talent and looks, I could be on Broadway. I could play all the big parts.

(As Maria from The Sound of Music.*)*

THE HILLS ARE ALIVE WITH THE SOUND OF MUSIC!
WITH SONGS THEY HAVE SUNG FOR A THOUSAND YEARS!

(As the Sailors from South Pacific.*)*

THERE IS NOTHING LIKE A DAME.
NOTHING IN THIS WORLD.

(Stamping his foot in time to the music and really belting out the big finish and doing a glissando up to the last note.)

THERE IS NOTHING YOU CAN NAME
THAT IS ANYTHING LIIIKE AAA DAAAAME!
I could have been a Broadway sensation!

ARES. *(Offstage.)* Brooklyn! Stop! I see you! Stay still!

DIONYSUS-AS-BROOKLYN. Oh no, it's Ares! And he's furious with me, he wants to kill me! ...No, wait. I'm her. I look like Brooklyn. Ha ha ha! Just let him try something, I'll show him who's boss.

*(**ARES** enters with a growl of war.)*

ARES. Stand in awe.

DIONYSUS-AS-BROOKLYN. Of what?

ARES. Of me.

DIONYSUS-AS-BROOKLYN. Oh please. You look ridiculous. That costume.

ARES. It is not a costume. I am the God of War!

DIONYSUS-AS-BROOKLYN. *(Flat.)* Oooh, how frightening.

ARES. Kiss me!

DIONYSUS-AS-BROOKLYN. Not on your life.

ARES. *I command you to kiss me!*

DIONYSUS-AS-BROOKLYN. Oh go suck an egg.

ARES. *HOW DARE YOU!*

(BOOM! Lightning!)

DIONYSUS-AS-BROOKLYN. Oh. Well. In that case, I've changed my mind. Come close.

> *(He does.)*

Closer.

> *(He does.)*

Perfect.

> (**DIONYSUS** *twists* **ARES**'s *ear.*)

ARES. *AHHHHHHH!*

> (**ARES** *springs into fighting position.*)

DIONYSUS-AS-BROOKLYN. Go ahead! Give me your best shot!

ARES. I will not hit a woman!

DIONYSUS-AS-BROOKLYN. You're darn right you won't.

> *(He pokes* **ARES** *in the eyes à la The Three Stooges.)*

ARES. Ow! Ow! Ow!

> (**THALIA** *runs in.*)

THALIA. Dionysus, listen! I can't find Ralph, so what do we do? Di...? Dionysus? What's the matter? Dionysus?

> *(She turns and sees* **ARES**.)

Uh oh.

ARES. Dionysus! It's you.

DIONYSUS-AS-BROOKLYN. We should talk.

ARES. You brought me here.

DIONYSUS-AS-BROOKLYN. By accident, actually.

ARES. You make fun of me.

DIONYSUS-AS-BROOKLYN. Well that part's easy.

ARES. I will kill you both!

DIONYSUS & THALIA. No!

ARES. *Ahhhhhhhh!*

DIONYSUS & THALIA. *Heeeeeelp!*

(As they race off, **DAPHNE** *and* **RALPH** *hurry in, calling:)*

DAPHNE. *Aleksi?!*

RALPH. *Aleksi?!*

DAPHNE. *(Desperate.)* Oh what'll we do! We don't have the manuscript! And I didn't finish the play and we're out of time!

(The **DEAN** *enters.)*

DEAN. Oh there you are. Thank goodness!

(Calling.)

Brooklyn, I found them! Brooklyn!

*(***BROOKLYN** *enters as herself.)*

BROOKLYN. Right here!

DEAN. Now where's the manuscript? We don't have another minute, they're in their seats!

DAPHNE. Well –

RALPH. The thing is, we don't exactly have it at the moment.

DAPHNE. Yes we do! I mean I-I-I translated it and typed it up, so then we locked the original in the vault, and here's the typescript. And it's beautiful.

DEAN. *(Suspiciously.)* Let me see it...

(Feels for her glasses, which aren't there; to **BROOKLYN.***)*

You read it.

(Reading it beautifully.)

BROOKLYN. "And as I fought in the light of the sun
That tips with gold the rocks of the shore,
I swore to the Sky herself, and to the Earth
And to the Sea from whence the Evil came,
I swore to save you."
Wow. Good stuff.

(At which moment, **DIONYSUS** *runs on, having escaped the wrath of* **ARES.** *He's himself again, but disheveled and out of breath.)*

DIONYSUS. Ha ha! He didn't even get close, the big blowhard. *(Calling off, to* **ARES**.*)* We'll finish this on Olympus, you hear me?!

(The **DEAN** *stops dead and gasps.)*

DEAN. Dionysus!

DIONYSUS. Hello, Marjory.

DEAN. What...what are you doing here?

DIONYSUS. I'm on a mission. Like I was with you.

(They embrace with joy and affection.)

DEAN.	DIONYSUS.
Ohhhhhh. It's so good to see you! You haven't changed a bit!	Ha haaaaa! Just look at you. And now you're a Dean!

DAPHNE. How do you two know each other?

DEAN. He was my first love. I couldn't resist him. I was in my twenties, studying abroad, and he came to save me from a life without hope. Do mortal women still fall desperately in love with you?

DAPHNE. Yes they do.

RALPH. Daphne?

DAPHNE. I'm sorry, Ralph. I couldn't help myself.

(At which moment, **THALIA** *enters.)*

THALIA. Daphne! There you are. I've been lookin' all over for ya to tell ya –

DEAN. Thalia!

THALIA. Marjory!

(They embrace with joy.)

DEAN.	THALIA.
Oh my dear, what a grand surprise!	I knew you were here, of course, because I've spent all day turning into you.

DEAN. And look at you. You're prettier than ever!

THALIA. Thanks. He thinks so too. And he's in love with me and he's really smart!

DAPHNE. Ralph?

RALPH. It's like a spell. Or a dream where it's all so clear for a moment.

DAPHNE. It is.

DEAN. Yes, it is, and I'm very touched and you're all very sweet, *but I have a band shell filled with scholars and the press and they're expecting the find of the century, NOW WHERE'S THE BOOK?!*

(They all speak extremely rapidly.)

DAPHNE. Of course you need it and it's a long story –

RALPH. You see I found the manuscript in the library –

DAPHNE. Just this morning –

RALPH. And I brought it back to the office –

DAPHNE. And he left it there –

RALPH. And I went to find you –

DEAN. And that's when I came to see you –

DAPHNE. Right –

DEAN. And you were acting very strange –

DAPHNE. Because it wasn't on the desk! And then, suddenly –

DIONYSUS. She called on the Gods of Ancient Greece!

THALIA. And we checked out the campus –

DIONYSUS. Which has the greatest hambluggers ever made –

THALIA. Then we called on Apollo, but *Ares* came –

DIONYSUS. And you know Ares, it's always drama –

BROOKLYN. Then *I* went to meet the professor myself –

RALPH. And we got acquainted –

DAPHNE. And I was invisible –

THALIA. And then I met Ralph –

DIONYSUS. And we made a plan –

DAPHNE. And I started writing –

THALIA. And I became *you* –

DIONYSUS. And I was *Brooklyn* –

DAPHNE. And then I remembered *Aleksi*, and I needed to find him!

> *(The following is spoken all together with mounting energy – and during it,* **ALEKSI** *appears at the back, wheeling in his cleaning cart.)*

DAPHNE.	RALPH.	DEAN.
You see I kept asking myself, where's Aleksi! We couldn't find him anywhere, and I knew by this time he was the key to the entire mystery –	And when she told me about Aleksi, we went all over campus looking for him, and it wasn't her fault, there was no one to blame –	I haven't the slightest idea what Aleksi has to do with anything, all I want to see is the manuscript and now half the college is waiting for us and we can't be late!

BROOKLYN.	THALIA.	DIONYSUS.
Well I don't understand a thing, including who the hell these people are, including Aleksi, but I'm telling you it's a terrific story with a great part for a strong woman –	I don't think either of us knows who Aleksi is, but earlier, we tried to make a palimpsest, can you believe it, I'm gettin' so smart down here, I think it's the *glasses* –	You see, as usual, we didn't get called in till everything was a complete disaster, but we had it covered. I had my *typewriter.* I was like *William Faulkner* –

DIONYSUS. – but then she wants to find some guy named Aleksi!

DAPHNE. So, I called his house, and his sister said – oh hi, Aleksi –

RALPH. Hi, Aleksi –

DAPHNE. and his sister said – ...

ALL. *ALEKSI!*

DAPHNE. Oh, Aleksi, this morning I left a book on the desk in my office and it's very, very important, and it's sort of red with loose pages, do you have any idea what I'm talking about?

ALEKSI. Yes I do, and I am very sorry. I am seeing book this morning, but it was not on desk, it was in trash and I thought it was worth nothing at all – that you had many copies – and then I did a very bad thing.

DIONYSUS. Oh no.

ALEKSI. I began to shred it, but then I saw that book was in Greek and I thought to myself, "Perhaps I can use this book to learn the Greek language" – but then I did something even worse and I am very sorry.

(They all hold their breath.)

I know it was wrong, but I kept book for myself and here it is.

(And he pulls the manuscript out of his cart. It seems to glow. And then a whoop of joy goes up –)

DAPHNE. Oh thank God!

(Bong. A bell tolls offstage.)

BROOKLYN. Dean Trickett, it's announcement time.

DEAN. *(To DIONYSUS and THALIA.)* Goodbye, my dears. See you next time, I hope.

(Embraces and goodbyes all around, overlapping: "Goodbye." "See you soon." "We'll be back.")

Ralph, come. We are in demand.

RALPH. *(To THALIA.)* Hey. I-I-I don't know what to –

THALIA. Go. They need you. I'll be back.

RALPH. *(To DAPHNE.)* Hey, I'm sorry. I guess I was...

DAPHNE. It's all right.

RALPH. Friends?

DAPHNE. Friends.

> *(They shake hands.)*

DIONYSUS. Does that mean it's a happy ending?

DAPHNE. I think so.

THALIA. And you had an adventure?

DAPHNE. I sure did.

DIONYSUS & THALIA. *We did it!*

> *(And a shaft of light from the heavens pours down on the two of them and we hear a choir of* **CHERUBS** *singing, "Ahhhhhhhh.")*

BROOKLYN. Does this mean I lost the movie?

DAPHNE.	**RALPH.**
Yes!	No!

DEAN. Would you please come on!

> **(RALPH, DEAN TRICKETT, BROOKLYN,** *and* **ALEKSI** *rush off.)*

> **(DAPHNE** *is alone with* **DIONYSUS** *and* **THALIA.)**

> *(Pause.)*

DIONYSUS. Well –

DAPHNE. Oh don't go. Please.

DIONYSUS. Hey, come on. You're ready for anything.

THALIA. You'll knock 'em dead.

DAPHNE. Can I go with you?

DIONYSUS. Oh sure. That would work out nicely. Zeus would smite me with a lightning bolt and I'd look like one of your hambluggers. Hey. Are you crying? Aw, don't cry. Look at all you accomplished. Complete chaos. Even I was impressed.

> **(DAPHNE** *tries to speak but can't. She chokes back a sob.)*

Listen, kiddo. We're comedy. We're right inside you all the time. You just have to look for us. And besides, you're about to peak at any moment. You wouldn't want to miss that. And we'll be up there cheering for you.

THALIA. Remember,
"There is a tide in the affairs of men,
Which, taken at the flood, leads on to fortune."

(They look at her, surprised.)

Shakespeare. He talked in his sleep.

DIONYSUS. "His sleep"? You slept with Shakespeare?

THALIA. I was inspiring him. Then one thing led to another. Like you and Joan.

(They start walking off.)

DIONYSUS. Who's Joan?

THALIA. Joan of Arc. Does that strike a bell? You said she heard voices.

DIONYSUS. They were *my* voices…

(They disappear into a mist that envelopes them.)

*(And now **DAPHNE** is alone with her books and papers. She hears a cheer go up in the distance as, presumably, **RALPH** and the **DEAN** are introduced. She takes a deep breath and makes a decision. She pulls out her cell phone and dials.)*

DAPHNE. Hi, Catherine? Oh good, I was hoping you'd be there. You can take down the ads for the two actors, I think we're all set. Well the guy for Jason is named Aleksi. I haven't asked him yet, but he'll be wonderful. And for Medea I thought…well, I thought I might play the part myself. Do you mind? I think I can do it now. I don't know why, but I just feel ready. Yeah. For a lot of things… Great. Thanks. I'll see you tomorrow.

(She hangs up. She puts down the phone. She looks up, inspired.)

"Oh I know you think me a timid creature in the main,

A coward who will never stand her ground and fight,
But shine on me the light of justice, and of hope,
And by the gods I swear I will not fail!"

> (**DIONYSUS** *and* **THALIA** *have by now appeared,
> looking at* **DAPHNE**. *They watch her exit.*)

THALIA. So what do you think?

DIONYSUS. I think that life should be an adventure. And if it isn't, go back and fix it.

THALIA. Exactly.

DIONYSUS. And we did all right.

THALIA. We sure did.

DIONYSUS. I knew it all along.

THALIA. Yeah, me, too.

DIONYSUS. ...We are such liars!

THALIA. Ha!

DIONYSUS. And now it's on to the next challenge.

THALIA. So stay tuned, world.

DIONYSUS. For the next edge-of-your-seat

THALIA. earth-shattering

DIONYSUS. death-defying adventure of

DIONYSUS & THALIA. The Gods of Comedy. *Ta daa!*

> (*With great love, they go out, arm-in-arm.*)

End of Play

> (*When the characters reappear at the curtain
> call, they swing dance to the music, just as
> Elizabethans danced to their music at the end
> of play.*)